Hex Factor: Classic Hardback Edition

SUPERNATURAL ROCK STARS
BOOK ONE

ANDIE M. LONG

Copyright

This book is a work of fiction. Names, characters, places, and incidents are either the product of the author's imagination or are used fictitiously, and any resemblance to actual persons, living or dead, events or locales is entirely coincidental.

No part of this book may be reproduced or transmitted in any form or by any means, electronic or mechanical, including photocopying, recording or by any information storage and retrieval system without the written permission of the author, except for the use of brief quotations in a book review.

The author, Andie M. Long, does not consent to any Artificial Intelligence (AI), generative AI, large language model, machine learning, chatbot, or other automated analysis, generative process, or replication programme to reproduce, mimic, remix, summarise, or otherwise replicate any part of this creative work, via any means. The author supports the right of humans to control their artistic works. No part of this book has been created using AI-generated images or narrative, as known by the author.

Copyright © 2024 by Andie M. Long.

All rights reserved.

Cover design and formatting by Angel Alley Designs

Chapter One

NOAH

"It's so cold out here, my balls are disappearing," my friend and fellow band member Zak announced to the three of us and half of the people in the queue surrounding us. We were waiting in turn for our audition for Britain's Best New Band, a reality show that could take unknowns and send them stratospheric.

Being a top rock band was our dream and had been for years.

"Are you not cold?" Zak leaped from foot to foot rubbing his hands.

"Idiot, I'm always fucking cold, I'm a vampire." I eye-rolled him. He was off his game today and I could hazard a guess why. The guy was knackered from his extra-curricular activities.

"Well, you must be cold, because you're not able to put your furry coat on," Zak pushed at Rex.

Rex didn't move, despite the shove. "Even when I can't have my fur on the outside, it warms me on the inside. PS, if you push me again, I'm going to knock you the fuck out." Ever the alpha wolf, Rex growled at Zak. "There are loads of women here. Go warm yourself up by screwing a few of them. Get some extra credit."

Zak's shoulders slumped. "I'll not stay awake for the audition if I do that. I need to have a word with Abaddon, seriously. My quota is too large. I could hack it when I was eighteen, but I can't now."

Roman, our lead guitarist, took a swig from the bottle of scotch he seemed to have permanently attached to his hand. "I feel lovely and warm."

"Fuck off, Satyr. That's because your blood is almost 100% proof."

"Can you keep it down, Zak?" I narrowed my gaze at him. "I don't think we should be broadcasting our paranormal status to the two thousand humans we're sharing the queue with."

"Excuse me?" A slim blonde tapped Zak on the arm. She was wearing a fluffy blanket around her shoulders. "You can share my blanket if you like?"

Zak ran a hand through his hair.

"Oh look, he's responding to the female. The penis flytrap is about to ensnare another victim," Rex scoffed.

2

Roman almost choked on his mouthful of whisky. "Penis flytrap. That's fucking fabulous."

Zak gave us all a withering glare, then turned back to the blonde. "Thanks, doll. I'd like to take you up on your invitation to share your blanket another day, if I may? Perhaps you could give me your phone number?" Then he yawned. It didn't put the blonde off though. She gave him a beaming smile and her contact details.

* * *

Five-and-a-half hours later, we were through the doors and waiting inside to see a producer. An older guy walked up to us.

"Okay, *The Para-not-normals*?"

"That's us," I confirmed.

"Great, well sing away." He looked back at his clipboard.

My mouth dropped open. "Here?"

"Yeah, here," the guy replied, looking bored.

"Okay, let me just get us organised."

The producer shook his head. "Nope, sing now. Yes or no from me, and then we're done." His fingers tapped his clipboard in impatience.

Shit, we'd better hurry up.

"After three, guys," I ordered the others.

We sang one line of Ed Sheeran's *Shape of You*, before

the guy yelled. "Okay, that's a yes. Here's your ticket. Go through that door for the next stage of the competition."

"Will I get to meet Carmela?" Zak now looked much more alert considering he might be about to share the same oxygen as the former girl band member Carmela Toto who was on the judging panel this year.

"You're joking, mate. She doesn't turn up until we start filming. It's another producer again. One higher up the food chain though." The guy walked off.

"We got through to the next round." I raised my hand up to the others, but every one of them left me hanging while looking at me like I was a wally. "I'm hurt," I told them. Things like this reminded me of my teenage years at school; times I did my best to forget.

"I'm still defrosting," Zak replied. "Oooh, they're selling coffee over there, thank fuck. Back in a sec and then we can go through and wait for another billion years, although at least this time we'll be in the warm."

When we eventually got into the other room, we had another two hour wait. Now I was starting to feel pangs in my stomach that let me know it was time to feed. As soon as these rounds were done, I'd need to find a willing participant for a blood donation. I didn't usually have a problem. Given I was tall, dark, and fangsome, usually I had women falling at my feet, especially after I'd drained them to the point of anaemia.

We'd been ignoring carnal glances from women and a

few men since we'd arrived and given some of them would be devastated at getting to this second round and getting a 'no', later I could give them a 'yeeeeesssss'.

This time we had to stand in front of a producer in a room by ourselves. The female redhead had the same bored personality as the man before her.

"And sing."

We began singing, our voices harmonizing, although Zak was the lead. The producer's face became more animated, a brow rising.

"It's a yes. Let me have your details and we'll be in touch about the next stage of the competition."

"You mean I don't get to meet Carmela today?" Zak whined again.

"Nope. That'll be next time." She licked across her top lip. "But if you're free for a drink, I'll be finished in…" She checked her watch and sighed, "about another six hours."

He shrugged his shoulders. "Probably a good thing. I'm exhausted. Maybe another day?" Once again he secured a telephone number.

As we walked out of the audition room, a runner came towards us with a tray holding tea, coffee, and water. As she passed by other people, drinks were swiped off her tray and by the time she got to us, she was empty. "Can I get you any refreshments?" she asked, super-enthusiastic. "I'll just have to pop back to the kitchen to re-stock."

"Yes, please. I'm parched," I told her. "I'll follow you there."

* * *

We didn't get to the kitchen. The show's runners were supposed to keep everyone happy and the dark-haired one now sucking my cock was doing just that.

"Yeah, baby, just like that." I grabbed the back of her head, fisted my hand in her hair and thrust myself closer so I went further down the back of her throat. Her eyes watered a bit, but bless her, she carried on like a trooper. Before long I was emptying my load down her throat. I looked at the runner's lanyard. Her name was Jan. By tomorrow I'd have forgotten it, but right now that shit was important.

"Hey, Jan, baby." I beckoned her up to me with my right index finger and she scrabbled up from her knees to come closer.

"Yes?"

"I think you have something on your neck. Let me see." I did my best concerned gaze as I pushed my hands, one on her temple, one on her neck slightly to tilt her head, so I could peer closer.

"What is it?" Jan trembled a little which made my cock harder.

"Me," I growled as my fangs descended and I bit

through her skin. Her lovely human blood sang to me as it rose in a merry dance into my mouth. I greedily took what I needed before my tongue licked the wounds closed. Jan's eyes were lust-filled as euphoria hit her system.

"Fuck me," she whimpered.

So I did. Bending her over the sofa in the empty dressing room she'd taken me to, I pulled her panties down and off and then thrust straight into her wet heat. She groaned as I took her further towards paradise. Being drained and given multiple orgasms did that to a woman. After I'd come in her (no babies from this undead guy), I laid her on the sofa in the room and whispered in her ear. But these were no whisperings of love, rather those of vampire compulsion to tell her that she was feeling ill and needed to rest.

When I made my way back to the audition room there was no sign of any of my bandmates. We were used to each other's different ways after meeting at college years ago.

Feeling on top of my game now I had recently fed, I allowed myself to get excited about the fact we were through to the judges rounds of Britain's Best New Band. My teenage dreams could potentially become a reality.

Leaving the building, the smug smile I was wearing slid straight off into my boots as I came face to face with a contestant making her way inside.

Stacey Williams.

My ex-girlfriend.

The girl I'd loved, but who I'd given up in order to pursue my dreams of fame.

Her eyes met mine and her mouth turned down in a sneer. Then she pushed past me, knocking my shoulder hard and was gone inside the building.

She was entering the competition?

That meant she was *my* competition.

My rival.

There was a fine line between love and hate and it appeared Stacey had come down on the side of vengeance.

The worst thing? I couldn't blame her.

I sped back to my apartment, thankful of my inbuilt vamp speed, sat straight down on the sofa and thought about how fucking delicious Stacey had looked. Long dark hair, a cracking pair of tits that her tight grey t-shirt ripped over the midriff hinted at to perfection, thighs that would squeeze the life from me were I not already dead. But whereas her green eyes used to sparkle with love, now they'd been crackling with pure venom. It was a long way from how we used to be around each other. But I couldn't change the past, and Stacey had every right to look at me that way after how I'd treated her.

I let my mind drift back.

Weston Senior School – eight years earlier

"Come on, choir. This is our last rehearsal ready for the end of year show. So pull out all the stops for me now and sing your hearts out. Pretend this is the performance to the parents."

Stacey, my girlfriend of the last year, rolled her eyes at me. The choir was where all the losers who could sing ended up. The ones where they didn't want us visible, but appreciated we had a good voice. All the adored kids had parts in the actual school play which this time was a production of Grease. Well, Stacey was my Sandy, and I was her Danny, so I didn't care.

Except I did. I was sick of being picked on by the cool kids at school. They permanently took the piss out of the fact I wasn't able to wear the designer stuff like they did. I had cheap non-branded shoes—the only ones my mother could afford as a single mum—and they called me things like Coco because I had clown feet; any damn thing to make themselves feel better and popular.

Where Stacey got completely ignored by everyone, like she didn't exist at all, I was a target for all. Sneered at, despised, told I stank, all because I couldn't wear labels and I had braces on my teeth that weren't invisible.

Finally, the bell rang signalling the end of the class and we pulled on our coats and left the building.

"Another exciting day at Weston complete." Stacey linked her arm through mine.

"Oh look, Granger's carer is with him again." Jack Brooks, my main enemy, sniggered as he stomped past, knocking my bag off my shoulder as he did. "Ever want a real man, come look me up." He winked at Stacey. "My mum said it was important to do charity work."

I hated the fact that I couldn't stick up for my girlfriend. The last time I'd tried, they'd held me down, stripped me of my trousers and pants, and tied me to a lamppost outside school by my own belt. I didn't know what Stacey saw in me.

"Stacey—" I began, but I saw her mouth twist in annoyance.

*"Noah, you are the kindest soul I ever met, and I love you. I don't want anyone else. It's their fault they can't see what I see, and it's my gain. It's their loss and that's because **they** are losers."*

I smiled a half-hearted smile. "I love you too, Stacey. You are the strongest person I've ever met, and the most talented, with the voice of an angel. And one day you'll get your place in the limelight, I'm sure."

Stacey squeezed my arm with hers. "One day, Noah, we'll show them. We'll be the ones on top and they'll have a house in Loserville. Together we are invincible." She kissed my cheek. "Now come on, I might even let you feel my boobs."

Now my smile became genuinely wider.

Maybe I could turn things around? I had one more year at this damn school and then college beckoned. Perhaps I could reinvent myself?

Truth was, I wasn't sure I'd survive another year.

Funnily enough, I didn't.

Chapter Two
STACEY

I couldn't say it was a surprise to have bumped into my ex. I'd known it would happen sooner rather than later. Appeared it was sooner. The Para-not-normals were extremely talented, and let's be clear, I was talking about musically here. But so were my band, The Seven Sisters. I'd fully expected both our bands to advance beyond the first rounds of the competition. What I hadn't expected was to bump into Noah just outside the building on the very first audition day. My prayers had been to not see him until we'd hopefully got through to the live finals. I'd have liked my appearance there to have knocked him on his arse.

His really fucking fit, tight as a peach in my gentle hold, arse.

Bastard.

He'd looked so good, and I hated him for it. That dark

spiked hair. His dark-brown eyes, like pools of chocolate sauce. You wanted them on you, like syrup drizzled down your naked body.

Come on, Stacey, stop this, I urged myself as we waited to sing for a second time. I was genuinely here for a chance to win the talent show and get my career on a high, but I'd be lying if I didn't admit revenge on Noah was a close... second. Yes, second... just.

Seven Sisters needed to win this whole competition, and although we were all witches, I wouldn't use a single spell to advance us to the final and to win. I wanted us to win on our talent alone. Then not only would my dreams come true, but it would show Noah 'fucktard' Granger that when he'd made his choice years ago, he'd made the wrong one.

His dark-brown eyes reminded me of how bitter I was still, all these years later. Like 100% cocoa solids.

I spoke to the rest of my band. "We have to get through this round. We have to win this show."

"You got it, sister! We're going to be the next *Little Mix*, but with seven of us!" Donna said with gusto. At five foot one she often jumped up and down a little when she was excited.

We called each other sisters as we belonged to the same coven. When I'd been at my lowest, I'd found solace in spells and had found the local coven. They'd become my family, and I loved them all as if they were my biological brood.

Though I smiled, it wasn't worn on my face for long. I'd never confessed the truth to my bandmates about the other reason I wanted to win. Mainly because at least one of them would find a way around the 'harm no others' rule and turn Noah into a literal toad, rather than the metaphorical one he was. So, it was my secret to keep for as long as I was able.

Until our paths drew back closer together as the competition progressed, when I'd find it hard to cover up my true feelings for the idiot.

I'd loved that boy. Not the man. The boy. Until he'd changed, and it had been a long time until I'd found out why.

Noah and I had dated in school for a year. He was in the year above me and I'd thought he hung the moon. I had no interest in the self-appointed kings and queens of our school and their simpering subjects. I'd recognised what a kind, loyal boy Noah was. We'd met when he joined the school choir.

Being in the choir was more time we could spend together. We made plans for our musical future beyond the choir, and as a duo. I'd fully intended to give him my virginity at sixteen.

But before any of that happened, he'd finished with me. The boy I loved had changed in front of my eyes.

Grown in appearance and in confidence. Instead of being the school joke, he'd become popular.

I'd waited, hung on, in the hope he'd change his mind. Because the boy I'd loved wouldn't do that to me. He was too kind. He must have been having a breakdown. He'd come around if I held on.

But finally, partway through my final year, I'd seen him, in an alleyway near the local tattoo parlour, with an older woman with dark brown hair. She was caressing his face with her fingers with such love. I'd turned and run back the way I'd come, tears streaming down my face, as I realised that it was really all over, and Noah was never coming back. Was not going to say he'd made a mistake.

Stacey Williams clearly didn't fit in with his image anymore.

At sixteen I'd given my virginity to Jack Brooks instead, who'd been sniffing round me in forever. A large error in judgement. It's not every day you have to confess to a one-night stand in front of your mother and two detectives when your one-off crap shag goes missing. He was never found.

It was a long time before I found out the truth about the woman with the long, dark hair. A drunken mistake a couple of years ago. I wouldn't let my thoughts go there now. I'd pushed the memories deep inside the locked compartment in my mind.

I shook myself down as if spiders were in my hair. My

focus needed to be on this final and in forgetting Noah Granger once and for all.

Once I'd beaten him and taught him a valuable life lesson of course.

That ditching me had been the worst mistake he'd ever made, and one that he'd regret for the rest of his undead life.

And that was a fucking long time.

Chapter Three
NOAH

<u>Eight years earlier</u>

On my way home after the end of school concert, I found the cool kids waiting for me. Stacey's mother had picked her up after watching her performance. No such luck for me; my mum had been working late.

"Hey, loser." Jack Brooks, the most popular guy in school swaggered over to me. Dressed in Hugo Boss and wearing D&G shoes, he looked every inch the rich kid, in contrast to my hand-me-down threads that ran an inch too high up my ankles and an inch too long at my wrists.

"I dare you to rough him up," one of his posh friends said, and I groaned inwardly, because if someone said 'dare' to Jack, he couldn't say no.

He laughed, looking at me like I was scum. "Fucking

pansy singing in the choir. Let me give you a hand reaching the high notes." He kicked me in the balls; so hard I dropped to my knees seeing stars.

When I opened my eyes, it was to see Jack's fist coming towards me. A sucker punch that had darkness descending. The last thing I remembered was being dragged behind some bushes and their laughing as I gave in to unconsciousness.

When I woke up, I was no longer in the bushes. Instead, I found myself lying on a sofa in a house I didn't recognise. A woman who looked several years older than me sat near me as I came around.

I tried to sit up, but pain had nausea hitting my system and I stayed where I was in case I might pass out again. "W-where am I?" I managed to croak out.

The woman stood up and placed a cushion behind my neck so that I could sit up slightly. As she touched me to help me move, I flinched as her skin was so cold.

"My name is Mya," she said, in a soft, and caring voice. "I discovered you unconscious in the bushes and so I brought you to my home. You have a black eye and some other bruising which would suggest that you were the victim of a beating or mugging."

It came back to me. The hate from the kids in my school who I'd never done a thing to.

I looked up at my rescuer. At her dark hair; her

almond-shaped, brown eyes; her full pink lips. She was enchantingly beautiful. Even her voice was hypnotic.

"How did you get me back here?" I asked, "and are we far from where you found me?"

"Err, a man passing helped to get you to my car, and no, you're not far. About five minutes from where I found you. Once you're okay I can take you home."

I'd started to think it was a little strange that instead of calling for an ambulance, she'd brought me to her house. Plus, she kept looking at me like she was studying me. I hoped it was in an 'I hope he's okay' way, rather than an, 'How many pieces will I need to chop him up into to fit him in the freezer' kind of way.

"I think I'm okay now. But I really appreciate what you did for me," I said politely.

Mya sat on the sofa arm at the side of my head. "Tell me about these bullies. I may have a proposition for you."

I wondered if her husband was an ex-wrestler or something and would beat the shit out of Jack Brooks for me.

"Gosh, I'm so sorry. I never asked if you'd like some water. Where are my manners." Mya stood once more. "Look, I know what you're thinking. About how strange it is I brought you here. Let me get you a drink and I'll explain. I promise if you want to go home at any time, you only have to ask. I've not kidnapped you." She laughed and it showed her perfect teeth.

"I'd love some water please," I answered.

She patted my arm. "Everything will be okay. I want you to tell me exactly what's been happening when I get back. I can't stand bullies. I was bullied myself in the past and so if I see one, I can't help but intervene."

While she got my drink, I reflected on the fact that Mya was not only beautiful, but she seemed to have her heart in the right place, even if she did appear slightly quirky.

I'd find out shortly that although her heart was in the right place, it no longer beat.

She passed me my water and sat next to me on the sofa once more and I told her about my life at school. It was so strange. Like I didn't want to tell her everything, but it all came out: about Stacey, about bullies, about the dare that had led to my beating. I know now that she used compulsion on me, but back then I had no clue that Mya Malone was a vampire.

"I'd like to make you an offer," *she said. By this time, I was in dire need of painkillers and had half started to wonder why she'd not offered me any.*

Turned out **she** *was the painkiller.*

"You say your life is miserable and you're bullied daily. What if I could make it that you became strong, desired, had everything you wanted, and even better, you could get rid of any bullies once and for all, easily?"

A life without bullies? Without being beaten up? A life I could live without fear?

"I'd say yes please and how?"

"*Have you heard of vampires, Noah?*"

My eyes widened. She was a crazy woman after all. Fuck. I'd thought being beaten and left on the street was bad enough, but now I was trapped in a house with someone who thought they were undead and drank blood. Where were the exits and could I manage to get to them given the pain I was in?

Looked like I'd fucked it. Life sucked right now, and so apparently did the woman staring at me with a smirk curling her lip.

"*I can read your mind, Noah. It's perfectly normal for you to not believe me. Just humour me a moment. Let's go along with me being a vampire. The fact is that I have the power to change a human to be one too. It's called siring.*"

"*Let me out of here,*" *I yelled.*

She came closer to me and looked me directly in the eyes.

"*Noah, you will become calm and not panic. You will accept what I tell you and make an informed decision.*"

I could feel my heart rate slow down and the mad beat in my chest disappeared.

"*Good, good. Now, I was turned myself in 2011. I didn't have a choice, not really, but it actually turned out to be good for me. I don't regret becoming a vampire at all. I've never sired anyone before, but I think being a vampire would benefit you too. Anyway, I'm going to let you access my memories a little so you can see how it's been for me.*"

This head injury was obviously more serious than I'd

initially considered. Maybe I was actually still in the bushes unconscious?

"You're not. You're here, with me." Again, with the weird thought reading. "To let you access my memories though I need to do this..."

She lifted my wrist and turned it so my hand was palm up, and then bit down.

Euphoria hit my system. A feeling I had never experienced in my life. I felt no pain whatsoever and began to see flickers of images and felt pieces of knowledge come to me. Mya being turned. Living in a mansion with a dark-haired male, being happy. I saw her vampire family: the Letwines. Then the feelings settled, and I just felt calm.

"The feelings you experienced, the rush, the bliss, are all part of the vampire world, Noah," Mya explained. "What you just experienced will not happen again as a human. "This is what I'm offering. Strength... transformation... an extended family. Protection for life, or should I say unlife. Now, take time to consider my offer."

She left me and did various tasks around the house until eventually, after time spent thinking things over, I called for her.

"Mya."

She came towards me. "Yes?"

"I want it," I told her. "Make me a vampire."

Mya asked me questions and I could see she wanted to make absolutely sure I knew what I was asking for. That I *couldn't go back to being a human. That I would be the first person she'd sired.*

"I'll need to call my own sire to help," she explained.

I nodded. Though my hands and mouth trembled a little, I was determined to go through with this.

A blonde-haired man arrived and introduced himself as Lawrie. He and Mya went into the kitchen. I could hear low mumblings of their conversation, and knew just as Mya wanted to make sure I wished to be turned, Lawrie was checking on Mya's own decision to turn me.

Then they both returned.

"Okay, Noah, time for Mya to sire you," Lawrie said.

I didn't realise that to do so, Mya would have to drain me to the point of death.

It took the next six weeks—which thank fuck, coincided with the school summer holidays—to recover from my turning and to adjust to my new life. Actually, life was completely the wrong word—my new death. I explained away not leaving my house due to being attacked.

Stacey tried to visit countless times, but I kept putting her off, talking via social media instead. I felt guilty about how I was treating her, but I was starving and surviving on bags of O-neg Mya kept me supplied with.

Thank goodness the whole vampires-couldn't-go-out-in-

the-day thing was no longer the case; although being a teenager, I rarely surfaced until late afternoon at weekends and during holidays anyway, so my mum wouldn't have noticed.

As my fledgling status progressed over those following six weeks, I became the full adult male I'd been destined to become. Mya tried to act like a mother figure, although to me she seemed more like a bossy older sister. As my sire, we shared a bond that would never break until one of us died a vampire's death. I could always contact her through our mind link, though she taught me how to close my mind and keep myself safe. Mya taught me all about being a vampire, and she showed me how to find blood banks to get the blood I needed to sustain me.

My mum was shocked at the change in me. One minute I was a dweeb, the next I was six foot two, athletically built, and looked in my early twenties. But I wasn't the first teen male such things had happened to. One of the lads in my class had done the same at thirteen and luckily, she remembered. I did keep seeing her staring at me from time-to-time though and saying things like, 'How can you be that little boy I gave birth to, Jeez'.

I'd left school, had passed my exams, and it was time to start my first year of college.

A new place of education for a new Noah Granger.

I needed to think about Stacey. Now I'd be back going

out on a daily basis, she'd no longer keep her distance while I 'recovered'.

But I knew we could no longer be together. She wasn't safe around me, and anyway, I needed to get used to the new Noah Granger.

The one who could now freely make choices without worrying about bullies.

I'm not proud of the decisions I made, but in my defence, I was sixteen years old and well, a dickhead. And I decided that singing in a choir was not what I wanted any more.

I didn't want to be unnoticed at the back.

I wanted to be at the front, but not quite centre.

My dreams had been of being in a band. All the time I'd spoken with Stacey about our future duo, deep inside I'd wished to be part of some rock superstardom, and now that was a goal I could reach for.

Love could wait. I thought.

Plus, the boy Stacey said she loved didn't exist anymore, so in a way I was doing her a favour wasn't I?

Selfish.

Selfish.

Selfish.

But teenagers are, and that's ones that haven't suffered their own deaths at sixteen and been reborn a bloodsucker.

So Stacey was out and my search for my new bandmates was on.

I soon found out, by the power of my newfound vampire enhanced sense of smell, that I wasn't the only supernatural who walked the corridors of Greystone College. There were other quiet kids who hung around in the dark corners hoping not to be seen.

That was all about to change.

<u>*A parking garage, three months after Noah's turning*</u>

I looked around at my friends' perplexed faces as they stared at the music and fitness equipment I had placed in the garage of Mya's property. She didn't need a car due to being able to whizz where she liked at speed, and so she'd told me I could use it. She'd even got someone to soundproof it.

"Time to become rock gods," I declared. "Maybe we aren't allowed to use our supernatural abilities in front of humans, but we can certainly use our musical ones."

"God, it's not fair. I'm the only one still human," Zak complained. His long blonde hair hung over his face in greasy ringlets. He looked like something from a horror movie with his scrawny frame and hunched over shoulders. Like he was about to slither out of a gutter and bite through your ankle.

"You can still use your God given talents—and a shower—to raise your game." I wrinkled my nose in disgust near him. "It starts today, my friends. Look around you. Treadmills, weights, a drum kit, guitars, a microphone. I've fixed them up the best I can. It's a start."

"Where'd you get all this from?" Rex asked, out of his pouty mouth. I was sure he was the secret lovechild of Mick Jagger, but I wouldn't dare ask his mother. As a wolf-shifter, she wasn't someone to piss off.

"It's what the ultra-rich have dumped in the last few weeks. Most of it wasn't even broken, just not the most expensive toy to show off anymore. I've been doing a nightly tour. Vampire sight, strength, and speed are no match for the refuse collectors."

"I hate that you don't need more than an hour's sleep." Roman yawned after speaking. He was a Satyr which meant that in his true form he had the horns and legs of a goat. On maturity he was likely to become a wild womaniser. Right now, him being horny was just his natural virginal, biological state.

He was right. I was lucky. The development of medication meant that my species could now be out in sunlight whenever we liked, and an hour's power nap was all we needed to re-set ourselves at some point during the dawn. It also meant it was not so easy to recognise vampires anymore, something else that was of huge value seeing as being awake all night and sleeping all day was a bit of a giveaway to any enemy. All they needed was a piece of wood to finish you off and a vacuum cleaner for the dust of the undead and it'd be like you'd never existed. Thank goodness there was a huge 'save the trees' and recycling initiative at the moment meaning wood was a hot commodity in London.

"So what is the actual plan?" Zak picked up a microphone and even moved the hair out of his face to look at it more closely.

"We're going to work out, and we're going to form a band. Completely in secret. Then we'll book ourselves in with a hair stylist and a clothes stylist and relaunch ourselves on the world. It'll take us some time, and we'll need part-time jobs to save up for the hair and clothes, but we're no longer going to be the victims, we're going to be the victors. Who's with me?"

"You don't need to work out or have a makeover. You just look like that anyway. It's not fair," Rex moaned. "I have to run about in the woods all the time to work off all my energy. I'll probably break these machines if I try to use them."

"Okay, they're for Roman and Zak then. You go jogging."

Rex growled and I laughed.

"What are we going to call ourselves?" Roman asked.

We debated different ideas for a while but nothing good surfaced as a potential winner. And then Zak said. "How about an in-joke? We're all paranormals; well, all of us except me. So how about The Para-not-normals? I'm the 'not'."

"I love that," I said.

"Me too," said Roman.

Rex held up a drumstick. "Me three."

We high-fived his drumstick.

So The Para-not-normals were formed. Rex on drums, Zak with the microphone, me on bass guitar, and Roman on lead guitar. The rest of us could hold a tune and provide backing or occasional lead vocals.

Of course, my vamp speed meant I learned to play the bass guitar in super quick time. Rex was growly enough that banging on drums came naturally to him; and Roman had been forced into guitar lessons at a young age, by a father who believed all children should learn an instrument. Roman was keen to learn how to use an instrument all right, but one that laid between his legs, not against them.

Zak would later lose his 'not' status, but the band name remained for a long time.

Chapter Four
STACEY

<u>Seven-and-a-half years earlier</u>

It had been six months. Six long months where I'd cried enough to fill several rivers. But the six-month anniversary was the day I drew a line through Noah and Stacey, literally, on my wooden maths desk. Scored it out with the pointy end of my compass.

"You want to go shopping after school?" my classmate Fiona asked. We'd ended up hanging out together over the last month or so. We didn't particularly have anything in common bar loneliness, but it beat being on my own. She helped take my mind off things given she was a chatterbox and rarely needed an answer to her incessant spewing of words.

"Sure," I answered. I'd been saving my pocket money

and birthday money and finally had enough to buy what I wanted for my newly decorated bedroom. I'd seen a beautiful blue and green dreamcatcher in a small store hidden down a side street in the city centre, and some gorgeous cushion covers in the same hues.

My mother had decorated my bedroom. No doubt in the hope of bringing me out of my lovesick gloom. To an extent it had worked, as she'd let me choose the colour scheme of blues and teals, something that made me realise I was growing up. Now sixteen, I was in my final year of school and needed to study for my exams, not continue mooning around over my ex.

He certainly wasn't mooning around over me.

In his first year of sixth form, Noah was unrecognisable from the boy I'd shared a year of my life with. In body and in soul.

I'd see him with his friends as his college was only around eight minutes' walk away from school. He'd grown to over six feet tall and he looked so much older than most. I reluctantly had to admit to myself that he seemed far better suited to the dark-haired woman I still occasionally saw him hanging around with than little old me.

My boobs were growing, but I remained five feet five. I'd never really bothered over my appearance, still didn't wear make-up, and now I kept my hair up in a messy bun. Wearing it down and long belonged to the old Stacey and I wasn't her anymore.

Noah now hung around with three other guys who he must have met at college because I'd not seen them around school.

They walked the streets like they were the fucking Beatles or something, having formed a band. No one had heard them play yet, but Rex Colton sauntered around with a drumstick in his hand all day, every day, and Noah now had a plectrum hanging from a chain around his neck. Zak would sing and hum to himself as they walked along and he could definitely hold a tune. The last one of them, Roman, remained the quieter of them and sometimes I'd catch him looking my way. He'd give me a sympathetic smile. That let me know that they all knew who I was—the ex-girlfriend. I ignored Roman, resisting the temptation to stick my middle finger up in his direction. It wasn't his fault his friend was a fucktard.

I knew far more about them all than I wanted to because they were all the girls in my year talked about now. If I heard 'your ex' one more time in a sentence I might strangle somebody.

Girls followed them around, giggling behind them and accidentally bumping into them. Occasionally, Noah would look my way, but I'd just turn my own gaze in a different direction. He just wasn't the guy I'd loved. I presumed puberty had hit him late and at times wished I had.

Last night The Para-not-normals had played their first gig at Rex's little sister's sweet sixteen. A few of my class-

mates knew Paloma Carlton and had attended, and it was all I was hearing about.

"Oh my lord, they could really sing. Zak is so fit and he has the voice of an angel."

"But the body of a devil, right?"

"They're going to get famous. I just know it."

I wanted to put my hands over my ears, but not so much as when I heard, "Sonia says they're entering the Velvet Throat Lozenges, Voices of Tomorrow competition."

Anger coursed through my veins, burning acid coming up the back of my throat. He'd promised me we'd enter competitions together. As a duo. Now it was clear—though I'd known it as soon as I'd heard he was in a band—I'd been double dumped. Not good enough to be his girlfriend and not good enough to take over the charts.

Jack Brooks walked over to me while I was in the lunch queue waiting for my cheese flan, chips, and beans, my ultimate favourite food.

"Do you fancy going out tonight? We could go watch a film or something," he said, leaning in a little too close.

I wouldn't have ordinarily touched Jack with a ten-foot bargepole. In fact, I'd have rather touched a turd, but I knew he had a dislike of Noah, and for that fact I agreed to meet him later that night to grab pizza. Hopefully, the rumours wouldn't take long to get back to my ex. I hope they hurt, like he'd hurt me.

* * *

After school, I met up with Fiona and we headed off into the city centre. In Primark after she'd insisted I bought a cute little jumpsuit for my date, she bumped into another couple of friends who started banging on about last night's concert. I made my excuses and left to go find the shop down the side street that I loved: **Wiccan do it.**

I loved the title. It was so kitsch.

Pushing open the door, a little bell rang and the scent of patchouli and sandalwood drifted up my nostrils. I couldn't put my finger on why, but it smelled like home. Sighing with happiness and contentment at all the gorgeous items around me, I wandered around the shelves and stands. I was definitely going to make my bedroom have this kind of feel to it. Sauntering over to the book section, a book called **How to Hex Your Ex** *caught my eye and I picked it up.*

"You know that's just a joke read, right? Us Wiccans agree not to cause harm." A female voice from behind me made me jump. I turned around to find the short, blonde-haired shop assistant there. She'd moved from behind the counter without me noticing.

"Oh, don't worry. I don't think witchcraft is actually real," I informed her, watching as the smile left her face for a brief moment before it came back. It wasn't the same smile though. The genuine one had been replaced by the 'are you going to actually buy anything' smile.

Fuck. She must actually believe in it.

"Sorry, that was rude of me. Should I say, I've seen no evidence to suggest witchcraft is real, but you know, I keep an open mind about things."

Her genuine smile returned. "That's okay. I'm Donna by the way."

"Stacey."

"It's just I can tell that you have the source within you. The link to the old ways." She handed me a leaflet. "We meet at six pm on a Wednesday after the shop closes. You should come."

I opened my mouth, but she carried on talking.

"Keep that open mind."

I nodded.

"I love this shop," I told her. "Have you worked here long?"

"A year, since I left school. It's my mum's shop."

"Well, I've decided to take inspiration from this store for my bedroom. There are a few things I want, if you can help me get them?"

Donna nodded enthusiastically and she helped me gather the mirror, cushions, and dreamcatcher I'd chosen. Then she showed me a few candles and jewelled candle holders. By the time I'd finished there wasn't much of my birthday money left.

Reaching under the counter, Donna took out a book.

Introductory Guide for the Interested was the very vague title.

"This one's on me for how much you've spent in store today," she explained. "Something to have a look at, and then maybe we'll see you on a Wednesday. No pressure though," she rushed out. "We're not a cult. Just people with a natural inclination towards the old ways. We don't turn people into frogs, no matter how tempting that can sometimes be."

I laughed, thinking about Noah.

"Yeah. Very tempting."

* * *

I went home and got changed for my date with Jack. My dad said he'd hang up my new mirror while I was out. I didn't want him worrying about me being out on a date, so I told him I was meeting back up with Fiona.

When I got to the pizza place, there wasn't only Jack there, but a whole group of his friends, both boys and girls. The boys just said hello and chatted like I wasn't anyone new, while the girls looked me over with curiosity, no doubt wondering why I'd suddenly become Jack's new interest. One of them asked where my playsuit was from. It sounded like she was genuinely asking, but the girls glanced between themselves when I answered, their looks clearly saying I wasn't good enough. That I shopped on the High Street FFS, so what was Jack doing with me. They could take their judgy stares and stick them up their tight arseholes.

After sharing pizza, one of the guys, Jed, declared his parents were away and it was party time back at his house. Though the majority of my brain was telling me to go home, the other part said to go to the party and see what happened. Jack had been attentive, putting his arm around me, and had whispered that he wanted me to come along.

So I did. I went to the party. I had a couple of vodkas for Dutch courage, and then I slept with Jack Brooks in one of the upstairs bedrooms.

Jack had acted amazingly gentle as he took my virginity. Then he took his own pleasure, discarded the condom, sat back and laughed.

"Well, well, well. So you never gave it up to that loser Granger? Could he not get it up?"

Even though revenge on Noah had been at the back of my mind throughout all of this, I was insulted that having just slept with me, all Jack could think about was Noah.

Standing up and hutching off the bed, I turned to Jack. "Thanks for a nice night. I'll get cleaned up and see myself out."

He was already texting, and I knew what it would say.

I was no longer thinking this had been a good idea.

When I got home, I placed my other new purchases

around the room, lit a sandalwood joss stick, climbed into bed and opened the book Donna had given me.

Maybe I needed to know how to turn people into frogs after all.

The following Wednesday I returned to the store, and I never looked back.

Chapter Five
ANONYMOUS

<u>Seven-and-a-half years earlier</u>

Jack Brooks was drunk. I watched as he staggered down the path towards the recycle bins where he was about to put the bottle of vodka Stacey had drunk from.

I knew because I could smell her scent around it and around him.

Knowing what he'd done, what he'd claimed, disgusted me. Bullying a guy was bad enough, but to take advantage of a vulnerable female did not sit well with me.

"Hi, Jack," I sniggered at my own joke. I was about to hijack him away from here. He just didn't know it yet.

He turned to me, his eyes narrowing. "What do you want?"

"I have something for you," I told him. "But you have to come get it. If you dare..."

He'd never been able to resist a dare.

I drained him of his blood even though it tasted of weed and cigarettes. Then I flew to the nearest tip and dropped him under an old pile of rubbish like the trash he was.

Chapter Six
STACEY

We were through to the next round of auditions. The part where we would get to sing in front of the actual judges. Donna was like a Jack-in-a-box, she was so excited. She had sugar daddy fantasies relating to the main man, Bill. Each to their own.

To celebrate, we'd all come to our favourite place, the Rock Hard Bistro. Anyone who loved music, loved the bistro. They had a mix of live bands and themed evenings, and the atmosphere was always positive. The food and drink were excellent and reasonably priced, and the owner and manager, Stu looked a little like Idris Elba which didn't hurt business.

On a Tuesday evening, the place was getting busier, but the music was background rather than the main focus, the food taking centre stage.

We'd ordered lots of things to share: nachos, ribs, chicken wings, pizzas, wedges, along with some large pitchers of beer and a few cocktails. I was usually quite partial to a whisky sour, but on this occasion had decided beer went better with the food.

"So I know you're through, but how did it go?" Stu asked me. "You reckon there's a real chance I might lose my favourite waitress and bartender?"

Yep, I worked there, and ate there in my downtime. I told you I loved the place.

I shrugged my shoulders. "We got through to the next round, but after that, who knows? Could be sent packing and then that's the end of that."

Stu tilted his head looking at me. To say he was only about five years older than I was, he acted like my dad.

"'Keep a positive mind. Negativity attracts negativity'," I mimicked in his voice. "I'll meditate on manifesting my success later." I rolled my eyes at him.

"You can scoff. I manifested my entire business and I'm loaded. Both in money and down my pants, so mock me. I'll stand throwing dollar bills at you."

"We're British."

He shrugged. "One pound coins would hurt, and then you'd sue me for a workplace injury."

I laughed.

"So when will I see you on the television and be able to tell all my friends I know you?"

"There are the live auditions after this. If we get through that it's then the judges' choices for who goes through to the live finals. So don't be advertising my job anywhere just yet."

"One day you'll make it, Stace. Whether it's now or later. You've an amazing voice and it'll happen for you, I'm sure."

"If it's meant to be right?" I said. He nodded, gave me a squeeze and went back to work.

I sat looking around at the rest of the band. As well as Donna, there was Dani, Kiki, Estelle, Shonna, and Meryl. We ranged in age from twenty-three (me) to twenty-eight (Meryl and Estelle) and in the main got along really well.

"So, Donna. What's your plan to ensnare Bill then?" Dani shouted across the table, her brown curls falling in her face.

"I'll bewitch him," Donna replied.

"You can't use your powers," Estelle said bossily.

"I'm not going to use my powers. I'm going to use my innate charm."

"You mean, you're gonna flash your tits?" Dani laughed.

"You betcha." Donna giggled.

This was why I adored them. The banter and the closeness formed by a bond of women who'd come together with a love of witchcraft.

Speaking of which, I'd make sure to put a hex on

Noah that meant all my coven sisters found him repellent. You weren't allowed to use magic for your own personal gain, so I'd make the spell to protect my fellow witch sisters from him sucking their blood.

Simple.

Britain's Best New Band was run by the same team as those that ran the X-Factor, and a thought came to me to make me smile.

Maybe we'd picked the wrong show.

Because Noah had the ex-factor and would soon have the hex-factor.

I sniggered into my beer.

That was not how this was meant to play out, but it sure was punny.

* * *

Two years ago – Rock Hard Bistro

"I'll have a glass of champagne please and the blackened salmon. What would you like, Aunty?" the customer said in a cut-glass accent.

I took both orders. It was a rare quietish night due to the fact it had been raining solid for three days and people were no doubt choosing to stay in and order takeaways.

After I'd delivered their drinks to the table, the younger one, who I'd noted was uber-stylish with her sleek *bobbed hair and gorgeous green silk wrap-dress, clutched her head.*

"Are you okay?" I panicked. The last thing I needed tonight was drama. I just wanted to do my shift and get home.

"She's fine. She has visions," the older lady said, as if she was stating the younger woman had epilepsy. It was a good job I was a witch and knew other things walked the earth than humans or I'd have been sending for men in white coats. "Ebony? Ebony. Are you seeing something?"

Ebony had been looking like she'd already had several glasses of champagne, but as I watched she came around. Then she grabbed my wrist, making me jump.

"You have to enter a competition. Britain's Best New Band. In 2022. It's your destiny."

I stared at her for a long moment. She knew I was musical? Or was this a hoax as you could take a guess that a person working in a rock bistro liked music.

"You need to listen to her," the other woman said. "My niece doesn't come to London very often these days. She lives near the beach in a place called Withernsea, so you're unlikely to get her advice again. Enter the competition."

"O-okay," I answered.

And that was that. The two women continued with their evening like nothing strange had happened at all, and I knew that it was time for my band to practice, ready to enter their first serious competition.

Because my destiny was there. Whatever that was.

Of course, I suspected part of that destiny would be tied up with Noah Granger. Finally, it was time to get my revenge or to put the past firmly in the past.

And now here we were, through to the next round.

I was meant to be here. I just didn't know why yet.

Chapter Seven

NOAH

We were through to the first round of the auditions with the judges. It was everything I'd hoped for and more. We'd spent years gigging and being talent-spotted, only for something to not work out at the last minute. The Para-not-normals had endured many highs and lows over the last few years, but now I hoped we could finally catch the break we deserved.

I wasn't being egotistical. We were that good.

If you'd told me about destiny a few years ago, I'd have thought you were a crazy person. But that was before I learned about the supernaturals living amongst us. Deep inside, I knew this band was meant to be, and I had three friends who meant the world to me. Were my brothers in every way but biological.

"The Para-not-Normals," the crew member shouted

to us as we sat in the seating area with hundreds of other people.

"Do you think their clipboards actually have anything written on them, or just make them feel important?" Zak mused.

"Nick one and have a look," Rex suggested.

"No one will be pinching anything. We need to keep professional. Now let's go and show the judges and audience what we're made of," I said sternly.

"What bit your arse?" Zak huffed.

"No one in a long, long time. That's probably his problem." Rex guffawed.

We followed the clipboard guy up some steps and backstage where Zak's eyes immediately landed on the blonde haired, blowjob lipped co-presenter Harley Davies.

"Oh my. I need her on my dick," he mused. Clipboard guy gave him a dirty look.

"Concentrate, Zak," I admonished again.

"I thought the presenters announced us and then we went on stage?" he replied, with a furrowed brow.

He had a point. When we'd seen the show on television, the presenters announced you coming on for the judges. Come to think of it, no one was filming either. Harley, and the other presenter, Dan Trent, were chatting in the corner. Just before we went on stage, I saw Harley look pissed off with something Dan said, and she stalked off giving him the middle finger. Hmmm, looked like they weren't as friendly as they would no doubt act later.

Clipboard guy turned to us, looking smug. "You audition for the judges in front of the audience. If they like you, you do it again for the camera. If they don't—if you're terrible—then you also might do it again for the camera. If they're not interested, because you're entirely average, you go home. Stage is set up for you. When I indicate, follow me."

He walked out onto the stage, announced the band to the judges and then nodded to us.

Walking out from the darkness of backstage to the heavily lit area and the sea of faces in the audience, I felt both anxious and exhilarated. In front of us sat the four judges.

From left to right on the panel there was talent scout Maxwell Johnson; pop veteran Marianne Moore, who'd represented the Eurovision Song Contest in the sixties; Carmela, who'd fronted a girl band, but liked the attention on her alone and so had left to present instead; and Bill Traynor, CEO of Deep Heat Records. Bill, the multibillionaire who could launch us into worldwide stardom.

All four of them looked bored, though that could be due to overdoing the Botox that the showbiz brigade were so fond of.

"This is The Para-not-Normals," Clipboard guy announced.

Bill nodded. "Okay, sing."

Once again there was no pomp or ceremony.

We began our version of Taylor Swift's *Wildest Dreams*. They listened to thirty seconds and then Bill raised a hand and stopped the music.

"Okay. Here's what's going to happen," he told us. "You're good enough to go through."

We all beamed, and Rex growled, "Yes," only to receive a withering look from Bill. I glared at Rex hoping he realised it meant *shut the hell up*.

Bill continued. "Make-up will change your image a little before you come back on. Also, I'm going to suggest a name change, nothing too different, just taking the 'not' out. You'll agree." He scratched at his chin. "You know *Paradise City*?"

We nodded.

"You'll do that first but not well. I'll stop the process and ask if you have anything else. Then you'll blow the roof off with Wildest Dreams. Okay, thanks."

And that was it. Clipboard guy took us back off-stage and through to meet the team from make-up and hair.

"Right, I'll leave you here. Congrats, guys," he said and with that he was on his way.

We all stared at each other speechless.

"What just happened?" Rex eventually muttered.

"I think we just got to see a glimpse of what really happens behind the scenes of a TV Talent Show." Roman sighed. "No one said the path to the top was paved with gold."

* * *

Indeed, it was not. It was paved with going along with a reality show script and we agreed between us as we progressed through hair and make-up that if it led to the glory of a recording contract, we'd do whatever it took—within reason. Like Zak said, he'd already sold his soul to a devil so what did he have to lose?

Hair and make-up parted Rex's hair down the middle so he had curtains. I could see that after this he was going to have to let off some major energy and probably hunt because I just knew that deep inside his wolf was growling for permission to take the hair stylist guy's head off. Zak's was crimped, and mine was gelled so much it looked greasy. They put clear round glasses on Roman, making him look like Harry Potter's older brother and then finally they dressed us in clothes that took me right back to my old days at school, pre-turning.

"We don't say a word about this. It's never, *ever* mentioned." Zak glared at us all. "Not one word."

"Okay, all done." The head of the department radioed through for us to be collected and then we waited until it was time to film.

This time Harley walked over to us and said hi. She

had perfect white teeth and gorgeous blue eyes and was the epitome of friendliness, unlike her co-host Dan who stood having his make-up retouched and shouted for her to hurry up.

"Sorry, guys. I must go do my bit. Good luck. I know it's all a bit smoke and mirrors, but it makes for great viewing and ultimately that's what you want. Thousands of people supporting you to win."

She went on her way, her arse bouncing around in her capri pants.

"Do you think they'll believe me if I say it's my microphone in my pocket, only I'm rock hard." Zak groaned. "And I've got to look at Carmela yet."

"Look at yourself in the mirror instead." Rex shoved him in the arm. "Not gonna score many chicks looking like that."

Zak smirked. "Now you know I can appear in their dreams any way they like. But you've given me an idea. I'll look at you and those curtains you're displaying. Thanks, mate. I'm already limp as days old lettuce."

This time as we approached the stage we were stopped and filmed as Dan talked to us, Harley standing alongside him.

"Hi, guys, so you're The Para-not-normals. How did you four get together?"

I talked a little about us having met at college and how we'd formed the band, practising in our spare time.

"Well, the judges are waiting for you. Good luck." Harley smiled and then we made our way onto the stage.

From there on we did as directed. Firstly, we sang *Paradise City* and had to look worried when Bill held his hand up and stopped the music. Then Bill asked if we had a different song to sing and we performed our Taylor Swift song. It was soul destroying (well to those of us who still had theirs) as the audience cheered like crazy *because they were told to do so.*

Then it came to the judges vote on whether or not we went through to the next round, where the judges whittled down the acts and got their 'teams'.

Maxwell spoke first. "I think you have potential. It's a yes from me."

Then Marianne. "You remind me of The Rolling Stones in their early days when we used to hang around together. Great times. It's a yes from me."

Then Carmela. "I like you. You have a great energy. Yes, from me."

And finally, it was Bill's turn. "I like you guys. There's something about you, but I'm not sure..."

The pre-empted audience began to protest and chanted, "Yes, yes, yes."

Bill looked back at the audience and then at us. His tongue poked in his cheek. "I think with a little image styling and some expert advice you could have something. One thing though. Your name. I'm not into it. I'd prefer just The Paranormals. We can work with that. Get you looking like you're too fantastic to simply be human. I think we could have a little fun with that."

We had to converse with each other a little while the camera kept recording, as if we were deciding on the changes.

"What do you say? Ready for an image and name change?"

We said yes.

"Then that's four yeses. You're through to the next round. Congratulations, guys," Bill said.

The crowd roared their approval as directed and then we left the stage. Harley and Dan met us again backstage and once more they filmed our 'reaction' to being put through.

We were directed away from the presenters by another Clipboard guy who told us we could leave and that someone would be in touch. I was about to ask if anyone fancied a beer when I realised Stacey was waiting to go on stage with her band. I ran my eyes over them all. Seven altogether and all so very different. They didn't look like a band, but then again, neither did we after make-up and wardrobe had finished with us. Stacey was wearing her hair down and had barely any make-up on. She looked so like the Stacey of my past that for a moment it hurt.

Whose fault's that? I berated myself.

As if she could feel my eyes on her, Stacey looked over and met my gaze.

Her eyes widened as she took in what they'd made me look like, and I knew she'd had the same thoughts I'd had because she let her guard down and clear as day I heard, 'Fuck, it's Noah. God, he looks like he used to, but older'.

Quick as a flash she blocked me out, flashed a look of fury at me, turned on her low heels and walked out onto the stage.

"Was that Stacey?" Rex elbowed me.

"Yup. She's in the competition too."

"Did you hear that guys?" He got the other two's attention. "Shit just got more interesting."

"I'll catch you guys later," I told them as I began to walk away. "I'm going to check out the competition."

"I'm going to check out Harley," Zak added.

I walked around to where the audience was, but I stayed in the wings where the crew would let us stand to watch as long as we were quiet. Carmela asked Stacey about the band.

"We're called the Seven Sisters. We're not related but we are such close friends that that's how we feel," she explained. "We got together after a difficult time in my life, and I'd do anything for them."

"Okay, if you'd like to sing."

Stacey addressed the judges. "This is a song I wrote myself. It's called Regrets."

Carmela nodded. "When you're ready."

The song began calm and steady and like a ballad.

Once upon a time there was you and me.
Never thought back then there would ever be
A life without you...

The audience were quiet and although they'd been directed to be so, I knew that Stacey's soulful voice would have had them enraptured anyway.

Once upon a time there was them and us
Never thought back then there would ever come
A time without you...

Her voice picked up on the *you* and it made the hairs on my back stand on end. Her voice was incredible and had only grown better with age.

But you took yourself away

Never gave me a say

Then she went into a rock style and her voice picked up and growled out the next two lines.

Didn't give a damn, when my life broke down
Just ran around all over town.

I knew this song was about me. And she had me in her thrall. I could do nothing but stand there and listen to every word as the lyrics imprinted in my mind and my non-beating heart.

I hope you miss me every day.
I hope you want for me to say
That I forgive you...

But my love for you went away.
Tired of the game you played,

I could resist you...

*You left me, not the other way around
I hope you enjoyed the new life you found.*

*Regrets
Oh yeah
Re-grettttttts*

*Secrets
Oh yeah
Secretttttsss*

*Our time is done
Now I've moved on
I'm here... ready to sing a different song.*

It then went into a rousing guitar solo before Stacey picked the chorus back up again.

Regrets
Oh yeah
Re-grettttttts

Secrets
Oh yeah
Secretttttsss

No time for the past to show up now.
I've shown I can survive without.
Regrets.

The other band members had played instruments and provided backing vocals, but my eyes were nowhere but on Stacey, whose eyes went straight to me as she sang the last word straight at me. She knew I was there.

Of course she did.

Where else would I have been?

The audience and the judges were on their feet, and this was not scripted. She was just that good. *They* were that good, but especially my ex. And I realised that once more I was in a position where my ambitions for my band were on a collision course with Stacey's life.

Phenomenal.

That was the word every single judge stated, and they were right.

I disappeared into the corridors of the auditorium lost in thoughts of times past.

Chapter Eight
STACEY

I'd dreamed of singing that song to Noah so many times and the moment had finally arrived. I hoped every word had hit him like a shard of glass, but I doubted it would actually do anything at all. He'd left me without a second glance, and I needed to remember that. I had to keep putting one foot in front of the other until the blisters he'd left me with were gone and I could move on without pain. I'd dated since him, but there'd been no one who'd come anywhere close to my first love and I hated him for it. Hated that for some reason my mind wouldn't completely let him go. Hopefully this competition would bring me closure and then I could get on with my life, being 'fingers crossed' the winner of a million-pound recording contract. Even if not, at least I could have a chance of moving on, with the past finally buried and a peace of mind I'd been seeking for the last eight years.

And maybe things were already changing, because at the first round of auditions I'd bumped into the lead singer of another rock band, and I'd noticed he'd also hung around to watch us perform our audition.

After we'd finished filming and we were making our way towards the dressing rooms, Drayton walked towards me, his eyes running up and down my body. But then they also ran up and down several of the other women at my side's bodies too. Huh. Didn't look like he was ideal future-husband material, but he might do for right now.

He handed me a towel so I could dry myself off, given that the heat from the lights was fierce and made you sweaty, and then he took the towel and passed me a glass of water.

"Thanks. You trying to impress me or something?"

"I know how hot it is on stage," he said. "But now you mention it, you looked hot out there in another way entirely. I'd be rooting for you to win if I didn't want my own band to do so."

"You're honest. I'll give you that." I laughed.

"Do you like me enough that I could take you out to dinner, right now?" He put his hands in front of him like he was praying. "I'll totally get on my knees if you don't say yes."

I laughed again. "Why not? Woman's got to eat, right?"

"Yeeasss." He punched the air. "And you never know, maybe later a man's gotta eat too." He winked.

Drayton Beyer's band was called Flame-Grilled Steak, an apt name for the five beefy men of the band. They were all muscle and long-hair and if he'd told me they were bikers, I wouldn't have been surprised.

We swapped numbers and I arranged to meet him later that evening. Then I went into the dressing room and got showered, ready to head home.

* * *

"We need to talk," a cold but still enchanting voice sounded out as Noah stepped out from an alcove.

"I'm on my way home, Noah, and I need to hurry as I have a date." I picked up my pace, trying to leave him behind me, but in mere seconds he was at my side.

"You can't ignore me forever. We clearly have things to discuss."

His hand caught my shoulder and I flinched at his cold touch.

"Sorry," he uttered.

"You're either telling me sorry about the fact you're so cold, or about the fact you had the audacity to touch me at all. But really, the word sorry has no effect on me when it comes to you."

"Bullshit, Stace. That song says otherwise. You clearly needed me to hear it, and now I have. I know you'll never forgive me, but I still think we need to talk. After what happened the last time we met, and I don't mean at the audition, we still have—"

"Stop!" I interrupted his blast of words. "Don't call me Stace. You lost the right to that years ago. And don't bring up three years ago because it's been a long time since then and that was what got you out of my system once and for all," I lied.

"But you're not out of *my* system."

"Okay, Noah." I decided to call his bluff because I couldn't take this a minute longer. "Withdraw from the competition. Your band can find another bass guitarist. Give it up... for me."

His jaw set taut, and I saw the fight leave him. "I can't do that to my bandmates. You know how it is. They're family. We've got so far. They'd be devastated."

"So why are you here then, standing in front of me saying I'm not out of your system? Do you think I'm going to say 'oh, no worries about dumping me, it's all water under the bridge'? Or is this just to let me know once more that you think I'm not good enough? That you choose your new life. *Again.*" I narrowed my eyes at him.

"Why do I have to choose? You have your band. I have mine. We can find a way."

I needed this man away from me before I broke the Good Witch Code and fried his balls with a spell. "Leave me alone, Noah. For good. I'm moving on and I've met someone else. I suggest you do the same. There are plenty of other females around the place."

"I don't want them," he said, and fuck me, if he didn't pout too, but I couldn't deal with another word from him.

"You can't have me," I said. "Regrets, remember? What a bastard they are."

I ran ahead of him, through the doorway and when I stopped and turned around, he'd gone.

* * *

I was surprised to find myself actually looking forward to my date with Dray. Though I hung around with the coven, I lived alone in a small studio flat in Bayswater. It was nothing fancy, but it was mine. I liked my own company most of the time, and playing pubs and clubs provided a modest and irregular income, so I needed small and cheap.

Noah waiting for me like that had put me in a bad mood, so when I'd got home I'd lit a Sandalwood joss stick that reminded me of a calmer, peaceful state, and breathed calmly and deeply until I felt like myself again.

After grabbing a quick shower, I dressed in black skinny jeans and a fitted red t-shirt and put my black hair up in a high ponytail. A quick spray of *Si* perfume and I was out of the door and on my way back to the bar and grill where Dray had suggested we eat.

Dray was waiting outside the entrance when I got there, leaning back against the wall, the sole of one foot up against it, looking like he was oozing testosterone where he stood. I saw one woman nudge another and nod her head in his direction as they went inside. Dray noticed too and gave them both a head tilt and a dazzling smile.

He was such a lead singer. Born to command an audience.

Whereas me? I'd found myself centre stage reluctantly. Put there by the others due to my voice. However, once I began singing, the audience and everything else just fell away and it was me and my music. It bewitched me, held me in its thrall.

When I sang, it felt like home, like everything was as it should be.

And I craved that feeling, mainly due to the fact that I rarely felt settled anywhere else.

* * *

"You look good enough to eat." Dray pushed off the wall and swaggered towards me. He was wearing dark blue jeans and a faded grey concert t-shirt of a Thunder gig from the nineties. It stretched across his wide shoulders. The guy was built.

"I'm hungry myself." I looked him up and down slowly. "But it's a burger I want."

"I can supply the buns," he said, turning around and twerking.

He made me laugh and I liked it. Didn't hurt that he looked good too.

I was surprised when he did the gentlemanly thing and held the door open for me. Then he spoke to the waitress who greeted us, and we were escorted to a table. I asked for a whisky sour and when they said it was two-for-one, I decided why not? Dray ordered a beer, and we checked out the menu. Or rather I checked out the menu and Dray checked out my tits over the top of his menu. His legs were thick and huge and as he was so tall, they rested against my own under the table.

"So tell me a little about yourself," Dray said. "I'm guessing witch or Fae, but I'll put my money on witch."

My mouth dropped open. "W-what?"

He leaned closer. "I'm a bear shifter myself."

It wasn't often I was lost for words, truly, but I found myself stuttering. "Y-you're a shifter, and y-you know I'm a w-witch?"

He tilted his head back and forth. "As I said, I was between the two, but you look more witch. The Fae seem to prefer their bright shades of hair."

"So I'm not only a witch, I'm a stereotypical witch?" I'd gathered myself now, back to my usual sarcastic self.

Dray pointed to himself. "I'm built like a linebacker, with long-brown hair, if we're going for stereotypical."

"How did you know?"

"I have a heightened sense of smell. It's genetically there for seeking out prey, but it doubles as a species sorter."

At that comment I snorted whisky sour out of my nose.

"Species sorter?"

"I can also smell arousal. My nose is telling me I need to work much harder," he drawled quietly and huskily.

I'd just taken another mouthful of my drink and this time I choked a little. I did not want to think about creaming my knickers and him being able to tell. No way.

"Could you just give me a moment?" I said, excusing myself to the bathroom.

It was the first time my pussy had been subject to a spell, other than a dry one.

Suitably reassured that I'd blocked off any chance of Dray smelling me, other than if I let him later, I took my seat.

He sniffed the air. "Cheat."

* * *

The evening passed quickly with plenty of pleasant banter between us. I did like him, but there was no way he was coming back to my place or I to his.

"So, can I see you again?" he asked as I stood next to a waiting taxi, Dray having opened one of the rear doors for me.

"Maybe." I smiled.

Leaning forward, he pressed his lips to mine. They were coarse, but warm. I let him kiss me and I kissed him back. He tasted of beer and Panna Cota. It felt nice, but that was all. Just nice.

God, if he could have read my mind, I was sure he'd have picked me up and crushed me against the nearest wall to make sure I changed mine. I broke off the kiss.

"You have my number. Use it," he growled.

And I did.

We had a few dates, and they were as enjoyable as this one had been, but I didn't let things go beyond kissing and a quick feel of my boobs. I did grab his arse—his buns were worth a squeeze—but I knew I was holding back, and goddamn it, I also knew why.

My ex.

Chapter Nine

NOAH

I shouldn't have waited for her. It was a mistake.

She'd quite rightly challenged me and what could I offer her?

Nothing. A big fat zero.

I couldn't get her out of my system and that was my problem, because after getting this far, I wasn't going to leave my friends behind. This was the dream I'd sold to them when I'd been turned, and we'd first got together.

I owed them.

I'd already abandoned one person who now clearly despised me. No sense in adding another three people to the mix.

Stacey Williams wasn't mine.

But my brain wasn't getting the message. Neither was my little brain, because it remembered a random night three years ago... when just for a moment, I'd thought everything might work out. I should have known it wouldn't be that easy.

* * *

<u>Three years earlier.</u>

"There's been a change to tonight's line up," Zak said, as we prepared to go on stage at The Limelight, a club in North London.

"So?" Roman shrugged his shoulders. "Nothing new there. As long as it doesn't affect us."

"It's a band called Seven Sisters. They're following us on. The thing is, I just saw the lead singer..." his voice trailed off as he looked at me. "It's Stacey."

"Stacey? Noah's Stacey?" Rex clarified.

"She's hardly mine, is she?" I huffed. "We split up a long time ago, remember?"

We went out on stage and like usual I lost myself to the music, forgetting all about my ex. That was until she went on stage to do her own performance.

The girl I'd split from had been beautiful back then, but she was now all woman. Her brown hair was now a deep purple and rested over plump breasts encased in a leather bodice. Leather hot pants hugged her arse, and fishnets failed to cover shapely thighs and calves. She was spellbinding. The voice I knew had matured and learned its *craft and Stacey sang like a powerhouse, the audience erupting in applause when the band finished.*

I couldn't keep my eyes off her and as hers finally found mine as she left the stage, what felt like electricity shot through my body at our connection. But then I realised it wasn't electricity. It was magic. As she came nearer to me, I could smell it on her skin, could smell it on the other band members. They smelled like rose petals with an underlying hint of sage. However, as she finally approached me and stood right in front of where I was, her hand on her cocked hip, the intoxicating aroma of adrenaline danced in front of my nose, along with the sweet scent of her blood.

I picked her up and threw her over my shoulder and walked out of the club.

She beat at my back and then when that didn't work, she made an illusion of stakes all pointing towards my heart.

"Nice try, but the only wood around here right now is tenting my trousers."

I did however place her down on the ground and I turned to look at her, my arms folding over my chest.

"We can talk now. Or I can fuck you now and we can talk afterwards."

"Afterwards," she said, and we made our way into the nearest hotel.

"I'm going to use you for sex and then this time I'm

leaving you," she told me, stripping out of her clothes and revealing that hot body in all its glory.

"If it'll make you feel better, then be my guest." I shrugged off my own clothes, picked her up and threw her on the bed.

"How did I not realise you were a vampire?" she said.

"Because you weren't a witch then. You were human. In order to protect you, I had to keep away from you." I let my fangs descend and I bit her nipple. Then I sunk myself inside her.

She arched under me.

I moved my head under her ear and trailed kisses down her neck, smelling the blood that sang to me. "When did you become a witch?"

"After you."

"Ouch."

"Don't flatter yourself. I meant I found my calling and a new set of friends. Not that you drove me to look for how to turn you into a frog."

I stared at her and arched a brow. "You telling me it never crossed your mind?"

"Well, maybe every time I saw you with that other woman."

I thrust inside her again. "What other woman?"

Stacey stopped me from moving and stared at me. "The woman I first saw you with in the doorway. You seemed very close. I kept seeing you together."

Smiling, I shook my head. "Mya is my sire. She made me a vampire. Nothing more. I've only ever kissed the neck of one woman." I licked up hers, feeling her skin goose bump beneath me. "Though I've bitten many to feed."

"What does it feel like?" Stacey gasped, and so I showed her.

I pushed deep inside her and then I bit down on her neck. I thrust and sucked, thrust and sucked until she came hard, her pussy clamping around my cock and making me spill inside her. I licked the bite wounds, closing them and moved to her side.

"That was..." she said, and I waited for her to finish. To tell me how good we were together. Maybe this was our fresh start now we were talking about the past.

"Okay," she added, pushing off the bed and gathering up her clothes.

"Okay? What do you mean okay?" I scrabbled to get off the bed, trying to work out what she was doing.

She pulled a bored face. "I meant it was adequate. I got off and the bite was a nice touch. I'll just go freshen up now, excuse me."

I watched, my jaw dropping as she sauntered away from the best defining moment of my life.

After she'd been in there a few minutes, my ego decided that this wasn't how we were leaving things. I'd have to continue fucking her until she admitted it was perfection. But when I walked into the bathroom she wasn't there.

There was just a hint of the scent of rose and sage and a message on the mirror written in bright red lipstick.
Fangs for the memory.

* * *

Even now, the memory came back to me like it happened just yesterday. That was the thing about being a vampire. Time had a different meaning. Stacey had left and at first, I'd considered finding her and begging for her forgiveness. Then I'd decided I deserved it all, and that if she'd really wanted me back she'd have said so. The woman was not shy. Plus, I had other thoughts and feelings of why it was better to just leave it be.

A day later a talent scout had approached us with a promise of a recording contract which we came so close to signing, until a recession hit and we were dropped like a 100% mortgage offer. The interest had been enough for me to distract myself from Stacey. That was the excuse I gave myself anyway.

Deciding we just weren't meant to be.

That she was better off without me.

Deserved someone who put her first, always.

So, I let her go.

Again.

Chapter Ten

THE DAILY NEWS

SHOWBIZ EXCLUSIVE

BACKSTAGE FEUD THREATENS BRITAIN'S BEST NEW BAND SHOW.

25 August 2022

It looks like it's not just the bands who are wanting to take centre stage this year. Our showbiz insider tells us that Dan Trent, last year's solo presenter, is becoming increasingly frustrated at being pushed to one side while TV favourite Harley Davies gets more filming time as they record the heats for *Britain's Best New Band*.

It's a step into the spotlight for Harley, who rose to popularity as the only female presenter of *Ride On*, the show for motorcycle enthusiasts.

"He's livid," our source says. "He's being treated like a support act after being the main attraction."

Our source went on to add that it's hard not to warm to and admire Harley, 26. "Her smile is infectious. She's just so nice and has the most dazzling blue eyes. Everyone loves her. Dan is threatening to walk out if he's not given the largest share of the co-presenting time."

You heard it here first folks.

Will Dan survive through to the live finals?

Chapter Eleven

STACEY

The acts had been sent to six separate rooms to await the judge's verdicts. Four of the six rooms housed winning bands that would go on to the live finals. Two rooms full of acts would be sent home. The live finals started in a month's time. The show had already begun on TV, and audiences were catching up with the audition rounds.

My throat was dry. This was it. Either my usual life, or the live finals was my future. In one month's time, I could be singing live on television with my band and be one of twenty acts battling it out for a million-pound recording contract.

Whether we won or not, life could change from that first live show. There were plenty of finalists who'd gone on to amazing things, sometimes better than even the winning acts.

"Okay, everyone. The judges are going live," we were informed.

Me and the rest of the band members held each other's hands.

The judges were sitting in a room in front of a table with photos in front of them of the thirty acts who had got this far.

Bill was the first to talk.

"Okay, so my team is up first. We've been battling it out behind the scenes deciding who would get which room. I'd like to congratulate this room who are now Team Bill." A countdown appeared on the screen moving from the numbers five down to one and then the camera focused on room one, the room containing The Paranormals. I watched as the room erupted into screams and shouts of delight and I saw the four guys hug each other.

Noah was through to the live finals.

Marianne picked her room next as room five cheered and whooped. Donna squeezed my hand as the first room to be sent home was about to be announced.

"We'll be okay," she said.

And we were that time, as room two became a scene of devastation as dreams were crushed.

Maxwell was next and he choose room six.

There were just two rooms left and one of those rooms was the winning one. I felt sick inside as the time passed, and they dragged out the announcement of the winning room.

Room three.

We were in room four. Three of my coven sisters burst into loud sobs as they realised our dream was over. There was just an awful silence in the room, other than weeping. The emptiness of misery and shock.

We weren't through.

It was over.

We had to go home.

The cameras who had been showing room three's joy suddenly panned back and there we were on screen. Devastated entrants about to go home, dreams destroyed.

And then it panned back to the judges and Carmela was sat pouting.

"What's up with you?" Maxwell said.

"I'm not happy with one of my bands. There's another group I wanted, but someone," she side-eyed Bill, "put them in one of the losing rooms."

Ears perked up all around our room. Was there a chance for one of the losing bands after all? "I'm sorry, but I'm having six final bands and we can lose two at the first live round. I'm going to go get my other act."

She left the room and a discussion ensued between the other three judges and I realised then that this was part of the act, part of the hooks to entice viewers. It was all a ploy.

Carmela burst into our room. Cameras following her every move.

"I've come to claim my final act," she announced. "Seven Sisters, you're through to the live rounds."

A huge breath of relief whooshed through my body and then the next thing I knew I was fighting for my next breaths as my fellow band members squeezed and hugged me tight.

Carmela also hugged us all. As the cameras stopped filming, she turned to me and whispered into my ear. "Sorry about that, Stacey, but it made for great TV. If it's any consolation, your band is my absolute favourite and if we play this right, you can win."

Then she walked away as if she'd never said a word to me at all.

"What did Carmela say?" Kiki asked me.

"She said she was looking forward to working with us," I answered, because after what had just happened, I didn't want to give false hope. Not when we'd just got a little back.

We were about to leave when Dan Trent came storming out from a side room.

"Save it. Let me guess, you're screwing her? You're certainly giving me one up the arse. You can talk to my agent. This is not what I signed up for. My solicitors will be going through every line of my contract. I will not share the stage with Harley Davies any longer."

He stomped off, swearing under his breath.

But he was right. He wouldn't share the stage with Harley any longer.

Chapter Twelve

THE DAILY NEWS

FRONT PAGE EXCLUSIVE

<u>DAN TRENT MISSING</u>

26 September 2022

Speculation is mounting as to the whereabouts of *Britain's Best New Band* co-presenter Dan Trent who hasn't been seen since leaving the London Landmark Exhibition Centre after filming yesterday afternoon.

Rumours of an argument between Dan and TV execs

were played down today as nothing more than a misunderstanding over recording agreements, with producer Everly Timms stating, "We hope Dan is safe and has just taken some time out for a couple of days. I urge him to get in touch with family or friends just so we know he's okay, and we'll welcome him back with open arms as soon as he feels ready."

There have been rising amounts of friction reported backstage since our first exclusive back in August. Rifts between Dan and co-presenter Harley Davies had seemingly turned increasingly bitter.

Harley was unavailable for comment, but her agent said her thoughts were with his family.

With the live shows due to start in a week's time, Cat Purr Productions, who own the show's format, said it was too early to comment on whether or not the first live show would go ahead.

THE DAILY NEWS

FRONT PAGE EXCLUSIVE

<u>THE SHOW MUST GO ON</u>

2 October 2022

Cat Purr Productions has taken the controversial step

to go ahead with its live shows in the wake of presenter Dan Trent remaining missing.

Producer Everly Timms said she had spoken with his parents who firmly believed that by continuing with the series, it would help to keep the search for the presenter at the 'forefront of people's minds'.

The last known sighting of Mr Trent was of him walking down Sandbank Street towards an old abandoned industrial area, known largely for drug dealing and prostitution.

There is no suggestion Mr Trent was involved with either of these activities, and CCTV in the area was not working at the time.

Harley Davies will present the show solo.

Chapter Thirteen

NOAH

I was a mess. All the times I'd hassled my bandmates about reaching for the top and now I was rehearsing for the first live auditions while internally having an argument with myself about whether a vampire, who would never age, should pursue a witch, who would.

Finally, I was facing up to the truth I'd buried deep down for years.

I was in love with Stacey Williams. Always had been, always would be.

But forever was a long time in a vampire's world, and the other reason I'd let her go after our tryst three years ago...

Stacey would not be able to have children with me. Vamps were sired, rarely born. As I'd exploded within her warm depths without the need for protection, I'd rejoiced just at being inside of her at last.

But after she'd left and I'd laid in my empty bed, and I pondered pursuing her, I knew I could never give her everything she deserved.

A happy ever after with children and real love.

* * *

"Fuck me. He's off in a dreamworld again. *NOAH!* Get your arse in gear or fuck off and feed, because if Bill comes to check on us and sees you spacing out, he's going to turn you inside out from your arsehole," Zak yelled.

I may have formed the band, but once Zak got into rehearsals, his adrenaline gave him laser focus.

"I'm sorry. Okay, I'm in the room now. Tell me again what we're doing."

Bill had told us our first song to sing. I'd thought he'd be here to encourage us and give feedback, but instead he was home in the US. He would Skype us later in the week he'd said, and 'We'd better have nailed the song'.

We were doing a male version of *Toxic* by Britney Spears. Zak's drawled singing was sure to wet the panties of the entire adult audience.

The door to the rehearsal room pushed open and a fresh-faced Harley came in. It was strange to see her with no make-up on, her hair in a ponytail, and her dressed in a pale blue Nike tracksuit with white trainers. Her cheeks had a healthy pink glow. She was naturally pretty, and I saw Zak look at her like she was an ice lolly, and he was hot and thirsty.

"Hey, guys. I just thought I'd pop into rehearsals today and see how you were all doing. Is it okay if I sit and watch for a while?"

"Sure, as long as you don't put us off," Zak told her, moving clearly into his 'treat them mean to keep them keen' mode.

"I'll just watch and keep quiet, promise." She smiled. True to her word, she sat on a stool at the back, watched, listened, and her foot tapped with the beat.

When we finished, Harley clapped. "That's amazing. Keep up the good work," she said, and then she got up and walked towards the door.

Zak wasn't happy. He liked women falling at his feet and Harley was firmly on hers. "We're about to take a break. Can I get you a coffee?"

"No thanks," she said, "I don't drink caffeine, or hang with contestants. Would look like I was playing favourites, wouldn't it? Oh, also, the police are around. I'm not sure who they're going to speak with, but they're trying to see if anyone can shed any further light on Dan."

"Must be strange, him not being here," I probed.

"Yeah, very. Okay, I'd better get on." She waved and left the room.

"She didn't seem all that bothered over Dan, did she?" Rex looked over at the door Harley had just exited. "In fact, she was rather buoyant. I mean, whether she likes him or not, he's gone missing. You think she'd be scared over her own safety, and have extra security, wouldn't you?"

"I never thought of that." Roman walked to the side of Rex. "She was in a great mood. You reckon she had something to do with it?"

"Let's not rush to conclusions." I attempted to stop their imaginations running riot.

"Well, there's definitely something wrong with her." Zak pouted. "Because I asked her to have a drink with me and she said no. Something's fishy."

"What's fishy? The fact there are plenty in the sea, and you can't land this one?" Rex howled with laughter.

"We need to keep an eye on Harley Davies." Zak chewed on his bottom lip. "I'm telling you, something's not right."

* * *

When we left rehearsals, we called into the canteen for the guys to grab something to eat and drink. For me, it was a blonde called Mae. I returned from the staff bathroom with a pink tinge to my cheeks and a pleasant ache in my cock.

I felt wholly satisfied until Stacey walked into the canteen accompanied by the lead singer of a band called Flame-Grilled Steak. She was looking at him and grinning, and he was looking at her like she was prime rib.

"Calm down, bloodsucker." Rex put a hand on my knee which was basically like fixing me in place with a boulder.

"Don't look at her, dickhead," Zak added. "She'll know she got to you."

I affected a nonchalant stance. "Stacey's my past. She can do whatever and whomever she likes."

"That why I'm holding your knee to stop you from ripping out his jugular?" Rex waggled his brows. "Look, pal. Just remember Drayton and his pack are bear shifters. You go for them and they're going to gang up and swat you off like an annoying midge."

"I wonder how long they've been a thing?" Roman pondered and we all snapped our heads to look at him. He took a drink from his coffee, which he'd topped up with some whisky he was carrying in his backpack.

"For God's sake, Goat-boy. We're trying to calm him down here." Zak glared at him.

"Sorry. But am I missing something? She's Noah's ex, right? He's moved on. He let her go, not once, but twice. I'm not understanding the problem with her walking in with Drayton. They look good together. I wish them every happiness and I also hope that their extra-curricular performances affect their live ones, so that we can take advantage. I wonder if swallowing affects a vocal?"

"We'll find out soon if you don't fucking shut up because I'll put my own dick down your throat to quieten you down," Zak threatened.

That shut Roman up. In fact, he started to look quite sick.

"Not without six billion washes of disinfectant and several rounds of antibiotics, stinkubus."

Rex's other hand shot out and now rested on Zak's knee to stop him from launching at Roman.

And that was when Drayton decided to look over at us, taking in the four of us seated at a table, Rex's hands on mine and Zak's knees.

"Oooh, I didn't realise you lot had a kinky threeway going," Dray's voice boomed out so the entire cafeteria could hear.

Stacey left him looking over at us and walked towards the counter.

"Gotta go, the missus is hungry." He pointed after Stacey. "We worked up quite an appetite this morning." He winked.

"Gah," I shouted out at Rex. "You should not be able to hold me down. I'm a newly fed vampire."

"Come on, Noah. Do you think I've not worked out your weakness after all this time?"

"I don't know what you're talking about," I huffed.

Rex let go of my knee. "If I mention Stacey the fight goes out of you, dude. Might as well change her name to Stakey."

I scowled.

"If you want her, then why not fight for her?" he asked me quietly, which for Rex was a feat in itself.

"Because it's not that simple."

"Is love ever simple? I'm supposed to choose a wolf shifter from my pack. That's why I stay single. You seen what I have to choose from? Most men have a preference over bare or Brazilian; my lot are hairy everywhere."

That broke my pity party as I sniggered. "Fuck, Rex. I need to bleach my mind."

"You're welcome. Now, please tell me we can go to the club tonight because I need to party."

"We can go to the club tonight." I high fived him.

"Great, just what I need, to see the boss tonight," Zak groaned.

"I'll have a word on your behalf. See if we can get this month's quota cut seeing as we need you energetic for the live rounds. If I explain about the amount of pussy that'll be available if we win, surely he'll consider a reprieve," I said.

"You think a demon is going to have some sympathy for the person whose soul he took?" Zak shook his head in disbelief. "How you've managed to survive since your turning is nothing short of a miracle."

While the others finished their food and drinks, I couldn't help but keep glancing over at Stacey. The other band members had joined them, and tables had been dragged together. It was a noisy gathering, but the sounds of laughter coming from there gave me a pang that hurt more than a bloodthirst.

"Leave him," I vaguely heard a voice say. "I don't mind him spacing here, but we need to discuss what we're going to do with him long-term."

I soon came to when Stacey's gaze met mine and narrowed on me. She turned to Dray and ran her hand through his hair. He turned to her, smiled, and nuzzled her neck. Closing my eyes, I wished for something, anything, to break them apart.

"Bloody hell, what's happening over there?" Roman gasped.

My eyes opened and I watched as two police officers walked towards Stacey.

"What on earth for?" I heard her snap at them, and then with a deep sigh, she got to her feet and followed them out of the room.

"What do you reckon that's all about?" I asked the others.

"Harley said the police were here to investigate Dan's disappearance, so my guess would be that it's about Dan's disappearance," Roman said, grimacing.

"No way Stacey had anything to do with that." I stood

up. "I'm going to help."

Rex stood up next to me. I felt my jaw tense.

"Are you going to tell me it's not my business? Because if you are, we're going to have a problem."

"Nope," Rex said. "I'm here to offer my assistance. Let's follow and see if we can do anything to help." He turned to the others. "You two stay here."

* * *

We made our way outside of the canteen and began following Stacey and the policemen from a distance. I had superior hearing being a vampire and although I wasn't able to hear things from miles around, I could hear through a wall. So once Stacey had been led inside a room, I positioned myself outside and began to eavesdrop.

Stacey's bandmates had also made their way outside, but a show runner had told them that they needed to head to rehearsals as the room was booked for that hour and that Stacey could join them if she got out on time. Once more, I could thank my hearing for that.

I listened as the police told Stacey that it was only a few quick questions they wanted to ask her, that she was free to leave at any time, and could have someone with her if she wanted.

"I don't need anyone with me because I haven't done anything," I heard her say spikily. Good to see she wasn't being any less Stacey just because she was sitting with police officers.

"Could you tell us about any dealings you've had with Dan Trent," one officer asked.

"All I've seen of Dan is when they have filmed us chatting with him for the show. I don't know him at all."

"You're absolutely sure about that? You've never seen him outside of the show?"

"Most certainly not."

"Okay. Miss Williams. Part of our investigation is to look into the backgrounds of anyone connected however loosely to the missing person. Do you recall the name Jack Brooks?"

"What's that got to do with anything?" I heard her ask; her voice slightly raised.

"Well, Mr Brooks went missing shortly after spending the evening with you, didn't he?"

"That's right, and I had no part in his disappearance."

"And now another gentleman has gone missing, and once more you're around. You can see why we're asking questions can't you, Miss Williams?"

"I can see you're adding up two and two and making four hundred and twenty-six. Do I need a solicitor?"

"No. That's all for now. Thank you for talking to us. Enjoy the rest of your day," one of the male voices said.

Rex had stood there patiently while I'd listened. "She's coming out," I warned him.

As she opened the door, she huffed a large sigh as she spotted me. "Not now, Noah, please." She stalked past me. But I was hot on her heels.

"Stacey, what happened with Jack Brooks? I know he went missing, but what do they mean that you'd spent the evening with him?"

She stopped and turned around to face me. "Oh, Noah. They say eavesdroppers never hear good things about themselves, or in your case things they'd rather not hear. I was the last person to see Jack Brooks before he went missing."

"He went missing after a party, right, so you were there?" I clarified.

"Oh I'd been there, at the party... and in a bedroom with him."

I felt my eyes flash red as I lost it for a brief moment.

"I gave my virginity to Jack Brooks, Noah. Not that it's any of your business," she spat out, and then she stomped off.

Chapter Fourteen
STACEY

Oh God. If things couldn't get any worse right now, the police were suspecting me of bumping off one of the presenters. Plus, my ex was trailing me because I'd just told him something I knew would drive him crazy.

"You slept with Jack Brooks? How could you?"

Oh, that was completely the wrong thing to say to me, and as I whizzed back around, I think Noah realised that.

"How could I? What the actual fuck does it have to do with you who I've slept with? Who I gave my virginity to?" I snarled. It was a good job I wasn't a vampire because his jugular would have been out and on the floor.

"He was the main bully of me through school. You know that." Noah had the audacity to look hurt.

I shook my head in disbelief. "You're still not getting this are you? You hurt me far more than Jack Brooks ever hurt you. And maybe I did sleep with him to get back at you in some way. I was a sixteen-year-old teenager and made teenage mistakes, but ultimately, it's not your business."

"How come you can make a 'teenage mistake', but I can't?" he snarked back.

"Because you're dragging your mistake through adulthood. You put me second and you're still not willing to put me first."

"I could quit after we win. Just get the band on the map and then leave. They'd find another bass guitarist."

"*HAVE YOU HEARD YOURSELF?*" I stood in the foyer apoplectic. "After you win? You're so fucking sure of yourself. There are another nineteen bands in this competition. And you're telling me that if you do win, you're going to drop the band? I'm not buying it. It would be, 'I'll just do this one tour'," I said it in a simpering, whiny voice. "Anyway, I'm going to do my damn best to make sure my band win this competition and that you're left with nothing but regrets, Noah Granger. No contract, no future in music, and certainly no Stacey Williams in your life."

The next thing I knew I was crushed against the wall and if the shock didn't mean I was overpowered, the fact Noah was a vampire certainly did. His body was up close and personal, and his mouth was crushing on mine.

And damn my fucking body because it completely

betrayed my mind as it quivered under his touch. I couldn't help it. My body remembered how it had felt that night three years ago and it wanted more. My mouth opened and his tongue snuck inside tangling with my own, until finally, as I felt his hard length against my stomach, my brain caught up.

"Aaargh," Noah reacted as my knee came up. He clutched at his privates. Then I slapped him across the face for good measure.

And, of course, the two police officers chose that moment to come out of the room they'd interviewed me in. They walked past us both, and as they did, one of them said. "Don't leave London, Miss Williams, will you?"

"Kicking someone in the balls does not mean you're responsible for the disappearance of a well-known TV presenter," I yelled, as by this time I'd had enough of everyone.

The police officers didn't even turn around at my outburst. They just carried on out of the building.

"Is everything okay?" Harley made her way towards us.

"Not really," I said honestly, as Noah told her everything was fine.

"Come with me to my private dressing room. You can take a break there away from everyone before you go home or whatever. You can talk or not. It's up to you," she offered, along with a sympathetic smile.

Thank the lord. I needed away from all the people here, away from the police, and away from Noah. Harley was offering me sanctuary and I was taking it because as soon as I got back to the rest of my own band there would be six women asking me a barrage of questions and giving me a headache.

* * *

Harley's dressing room was down a private corridor at the back of the auditorium. There was a comfy red velvet sofa; a large dressing table and mirror, with a red velvet stool in front of it; and a rail full of clothes at the far end. There was also a fridge and a trolley full of goodies, plus glasses, mugs, etc. As I walked inside, it smelled of Harley's signature perfume, like sherbet.

"I love it in here. I'd never want to leave," I told her, sinking into the luxurious softness of the red sofa and thinking that when I had enough money saved, I needed one for my apartment. Oh, who was I kidding? It would probably cost two months' rent.

"Believe me, luxury only seems luxurious when you're not used to it," Harley said, and I noted the sadness in her tone. "I've always wanted to be famous, yet now things finally seem to be coming together for me, I'm lonelier than ever. Plus, now I'm being suspected of being behind my co-presenter's disappearance because they think I'd do that to get this gig on my own." She sighed and dropped onto the seat in front of her dressing table.

"They think you're responsible for Dan's disappearance?"

She shrugged her shoulders. "They didn't accuse me outright, but the underlying tone was that because it was known we didn't get along and that Dan seemed jealous of me, I might have motive." She stood up and opened a bottle of white wine. "Want one?"

"Why not?"

She handed me the glass and sat back down. "So I heard what they said to you about you not leaving London. What was that all about?"

I debated telling Harley for a moment, because what if she had bumped Dan off and then tried to frame me?

You're being utterly ridiculous, I told myself.

"When I was sixteen, the boy I slept with went missing. The police have found this out and so because of that and the fact I'm yet again in the vicinity of someone who's gone missing, I seem to be a person of interest."

"That's ridiculous. You live in London where tons of people go missing. Have you been responsible for all of them?" She took a sip of her wine. "Dan's a twat and he's probably sitting in five-star luxury accommodation somewhere, with a spy camera on me, laughing his head off, and planning his return for the quarter-finals where he'll get all the attention. That's how he is."

I giggled.

"Is it bad I just said that when he could have actually been hurt?" she asked me.

"No. We don't have to like people, do we? I'd find it a lot more insincere if you were doing some dramatic 'oh where is my co-presenter' fawning to the reporters."

"Don't get me wrong, I hope he is okay. I'm not that mean. But he's been super horrible to me and continually trying to get me fired, so I'm not going to pretend I'm devastated."

"Good for you." I took a large glug of my wine. I wasn't a huge wine drinker, but this was nice. Fruity and smooth. I could see it going down well.

"So, tell me about you and Noah Granger."

My mouth parted in an 'O'.

"I saw him plant one on you and at first it didn't look like you were too disappointed. Then you nailed him in the nuts."

"He's my ex."

Her eyes widened at the potential gossip there. "Ooooohhh."

"From school. I dated him from being fifteen to sixteen. He was a year older. Then he dumped me for his band. The one he's entered the competition with."

"Oh boy. This just got interesting. And do you still like him?"

"Truthfully? I can't deny there's still something

between us. But it's not happening. I'm going to do my utmost to win this competition: for my band, my future, and for the sheer satisfaction of hurting Noah Granger as much as he hurt me."

"Oh?"

"No contract, no Stacey. Just a heap of regret. That's what Noah's future needs."

"Harsh."

"It's no less than he deserves."

"Only you know the answer to that, but it'll certainly give me something to stop the boredom setting in. I can watch the real competition now. Noah versus Stacey."

"Glad I can be of entertainment," I said sarcastically. "Anyway, what about you? Got your eye on any of the talent here?"

"Huh. I can't go there. For one thing I'd be accused of giving someone a helping hand, and how do I know if they're trying to score with me to get further on in the competition? So, I'll just have to stay my single self for now."

"I never thought of that. That sucks."

"Hey, I'm the career woman remember? Determined to get to the top, even making my co-presenter disappear. If you want a new friend, I'm available. Because you're a suspect too, so we have a lot in common." She sniggered.

I held out my glass towards hers in a toast. "To new friendships and to sisters doing it for themselves."

She clinked her glass against mine. "So now tell me about Dray because I've seen him hanging around you like a dog on heat."

I sighed. "I like Dray. We've been dating. I've kept it all second base and fun though because he flirts with other women. The guy is clearly not a one-woman man, and while I'm not averse to a bit of fun, I'm concentrating on the competition from a musical rival standpoint, not a romantic one."

It was true. I had zero interest in climbing between the sheets with anyone right now. I wondered if Noah was the same.

Stop thinking about Noah.

"If you could date anyone from one of the bands, who would you go for? I promise not to tell. Only I feel you know far more about me than I do you," I asked her.

"That's because I'm so boring." Harley laughed. "Actually, I quite like one of Noah's friends."

"Oooh, who? Let me guess. Zak. Everyone gets the hots for Zak."

She turned her face up. "Not me. He's too much. One minute he's being rude to me, one minute nice. Far too high maintenance. I like a quiet man. I think Roman's really cute."

"Roman, huh?"

She raised a brow at me. "Don't you dare try any

matchmaking shit. I can't date them. Not as presenter of the show. I'm serious."

I held up my hand. "I swear I won't do anything…" I trailed off. "…while the show's happening, but after… well, I can't promise."

She laughed.

"Oh." I thought out loud. "If you can't be seen to be hanging around with contestants, doesn't that mean people could say I was trying to get a helping hand?"

Harley's smile dropped clean off her face.

"Oh fuck. I never thought of that." A deep sadness hit her features. "Thanks for the gossip and the drink. Maybe we can be friends after the show finishes?"

"I'd like that," I told her honestly. I passed her a card with my phone number on it. "If you need a friend, call me, okay? Fuck the media."

"Stacey?"

"Yes?"

"Think carefully about the competition. It's going to lead to fame and with that comes a price. There's more to life than an amazing dressing room."

"Are you considering quitting?"

"No. I'm not cut out for a boring, ordinary life. One day, hopefully, I can find some happy medium between fame and a family, but for now I'm pushing through until I'm the household name I always wanted to be."

"A happy medium. That sounds good." I left her

dressing room, feeling sad that we couldn't hang together because I liked Harley. What I didn't know was I was going from *talking* about a happy medium to meeting one.

* * *

The rest of the coven sisters had left by the time I finally exited the building, and there was also no sign of Noah, or Dray.

Good. I fancied a hot bath and an early night.

I soon saw that wasn't going to be happening though when I found Donna at my door.

"Finally. I've been messaging you. I was worried. Where have you been all this time?" She did look worried as well, bless her. She was rubbing her face and clasping her hands.

I took my phone out of my bag. Dead battery. "Oh shoot, my phone ran down. I'm so sorry. It's been one heck of a busy day."

"The last time I saw you the police had escorted you out of the canteen. I thought they'd flung you in a cell."

I laughed. "No, thank God. Anyway, I appreciate you looking out for me. Do you want a hot drink before you go?" It was a hint I needed time to myself, and I'd thought it was pretty clear.

"Yes, and then I want you to tell me everything that's happening. We're all worried about you."

Inwardly, I let out a heavy sigh. Outwardly, I smiled and invited her in. Then while we enjoyed a coffee, I told her about the police and about Jack Brooks. I didn't tell her about Noah, or about Harley, as although we were all close, I was getting fed up of everyone knowing everything about me.

I was starting to crave space and alone time. Things were changing within me, and I wasn't sure how I felt about it. Harley's statement about if I was sure this was what I wanted was weighing deep, and possibly why I felt I needed a bath and some space. Time to think.

"As if you'd do anything to harm anyone. We need to know if we're around danger though, so I brought some things with me." Donna reached around for her backpack and opened it up. "We'll start with a protection spell and then I'm going to demonstrate my new talent, because I have a secret." She smiled coyly.

"Oh yeah?"

"I've been practicing mediumship," she told me matter-of-factly like she'd been learning Spanish.

"Pardon?"

"I've been practicing mediumship."

"Under whose guidance?"

Donna's voice and demeanour got haughty. "I

borrowed two books from the library. I know about protecting myself."

"We know about spells and protecting ourselves from the harm of spells. Not from the harm of wayward spirits," I reminded her.

"That's why I got books from the library. They told me what to do. It's all fine. Stop panicking. I know I'm small, but I do sometimes get a little frustrated when you talk to me like I'm a baby. I'm a year older than you and brought you into this fold, remember?" She scowled.

Oh God. I'd really fucked her off and she'd just been concerned for me earlier.

"I'm sorry, Donna. It's just been a stressful day. I think it's great that you're trying to add another string to your bow as it were."

Her face relaxed. "Thanks. So I'll get everything prepared and then reach out. I was going to see if I could contact Dan Trent because then we'd know he was dead, but I can also try to contact Jack Brooks too. If they don't answer, we know they're alive and well."

Or you can't contact the dead because you've tried to learn through **Mediumship for Dummies** *or something similar,* I wanted to add, but didn't as otherwise I'd be the dead one.

It therefore transpired that rather than enjoying a hot bath, instead, I had to move my coffee table off my grey rug—the only decent thing I owned and that covered up a threadbare carpet—so she could lay out Scrabble letters in a Ouija style arrangement on top of an upside-down Monopoly Board. I daren't question her about any of it because I'd opened my mouth once to ask if we were going to have a 'yes, no, and a proceed to go', and she'd not found it as amusing as I had.

"Okay, everything we need is now here. As you can clearly see we don't have a glass out because we aren't having a séance. Through mediumship I will invite anyone to talk through me. The letters are laid out simply to let the spirits know that we are open to communication."

I needed a glass out and to commune with spirits, but vodka and whisky were my preferred options.

"Okay. Please sit with me and hold my hand. When I have said the spell, you can let go. We don't need to remain tethered in the real world as we will still be tethered in the astral realm. Time for a protection spell."

I was really unsure about this, but I'd known Donna a long time and she was a very competent witch, so against my better judgement I sat and held her hands.

"Goddess of darkness, Goddess of Light.
Trust in me with your blessed sight.
Protect both of us here tonight; have our back.
But let me be a conduit for Dan and Jack."

. . .

She let go of my hand and we waited. And then we waited some more. Five minutes passed and Donna began to look glum. "Huh, no one wants to talk to me."

"Erm, don't you like have to ask them or call to them?" I offered.

She slapped a hand across her mouth. "Of course, silly me. I forgot!"

Sitting cross-legged she closed her eyes and spoke. "Dan Trent from the television show Britain's Best New Band. Are you there?"

There was no reply, so she tried Jack.

"Jack Brooks, who slept with my friend, Stacey Williams. Are you there?"

Again, nothing happened, and I was truly tired and fed up now. I wanted my bath, and I wanted my friend to leave.

"Let's leave this, shall we?" I suggested.

Then Donna's eyes went jet black, and her head cocked towards mine.

"You like leaving, don't you, Stacey?" a weird, croaky voice came out of Donna's mouth and a small trail of blood slipped from her left nostril.

I scrabbled back a foot in shock.

"You left me last time and I came looking for you. It's your fault I'm dead, bitch." Newly possessed Donna looked around the apartment slowly, her skin a pale grey that showed veins underneath. "I thought you'd do better for yourself than this, Stacey, but it's better than where I'm stuck. Where I'm stuck is complete garbage."

He leaped forward.

"You need to help me, Stacey." Donna pitched forward further but then jerked and her colour came back to normal. Gasping for breath, she retched and threw up all over my prized rug. There was no way I was keeping it any longer anyway. It had that weird blood on it.

"I f-felt him, Stacey. He's passed. Jack was murdered." She shook. "He's gone now. He tried to touch you and it's not allowed, so he was cast out. Can I have a glass of water and then I'm going to go home. I need to go think about the picture I saw in my head. Where his body might be."

My voice rose in pitch. "I don't like any of this, Donna. I mean, what happened was some scary shit. You went a weird as fuck colour, your nose bled, and you talked strangely. Please don't do it again, will you?"

"I do feel a bit woozy. Maybe I'd be better off practicing piano. I was between the two."

Heading to the kitchen on now shaky legs, I returned with a glass of water for my friend. Her colour was fully returned, and she looked better than I reckoned I did. "Look. It's not going to hold up in court, is it? That you saw a vision. Why not just forget about it all?"

Donna's mouth twisted. "I will try to find the place

Jack showed me he was dumped. I didn't get a clear picture, but it smelled vile. But if I can't bring the images forward then I'll just have to let it go. Hey, at least it looks like Dan Trent is still alive, because he didn't answer." She smiled.

"Great. Jack's dead, Dan's alive. All's sorted and now you can go home, because after all this I need a bath and a stiff—"

"Cock?" Donna asked.

"Drink," I corrected her.

"I don't understand you. Drayton would be round in a flash if you called him, but you'd rather have a brandy. Who ditches randy for brandy? You're not normal."

She eventually packed everything into her backpack and left.

Once she'd gone, I picked up my once beautiful rug and threw it down the rubbish chute, and then I went and got in the bath.

Had she really contacted Jack Brooks?

I mean, I suspected he was dead because I'd never seen him again.

Even though I'd seen spells performed and I knew of the supernatural, I was finding it hard to accept that Jack from school had spoken through Donna, but why not? And if so, then I'd actually missed the main question I wanted to ask him.

But if I got the chance again, would I *really* want to know whether Noah had been the one to end his existence?

Chapter Fifteen

DAN

Stupid dozy bitch.

Dan had not been dead long. In fact, he was only just getting used to the idea that he'd been bled dry by more than just his agent. But he'd always been savvy. It was how he'd kept ahead of his rivals in the entertainment industry. Until that bitch. Harley fucking Davies, with her sweet smile and no doubt even sweeter pussy, had come along. He'd put money on the fact that she was getting her top position from getting in an on-top position.

While his unsettled spirit wandered around the auditorium where he'd once ruled, his body rotted somewhere that smelled indescribably bad. No one had heard his cries for help. Even if he had been audible, there were twenty bands practising for a start.

He'd heard his name be called, and suddenly, he was

there in that small woman's body. He'd recognized the woman sat opposite him from the audition interviews because she had great breasts. Dan had had a hard time not reaching forward to feel one. You were a long time dead after all. But no, he knew that the woman who'd called him could just as easily cast him away, so he lingered to see what would happen. And what did happen? She called on someone else. There wasn't room for the two of them, I mean three's a crowd, right? So as soon as the other guy entered her, he got ejected. It was the first threesome where he was glad another guy got the girl. So now there he was, back where he'd been hanging around, at the auditorium, but now it seemed he could pop where he liked. And of course, he knew that his rightful place was presenting a top television series.

Dan Trent's spirit went looking for Harley.

He was going to take over the show in more ways than one.

Chapter Sixteen

NOAH

"Well, mate, I think it's good we're going to the club tonight, so you can talk to me about what the heck is going on with you and your ex, and why you just almost banged her in the corridor." Rex fixed me with a look that said, 'you will tell me all'.

"We're men. We don't talk feelings and shit. She kneed me in the balls and made it clear we're most definitely done. That and her being with Drayton. I had a lapse of sense because my blood had diverted south. There's nothing else to say." I stalked off ahead of him and left the building.

"I'll see you at the club at ten," Rex said. "You'd better be there."

"I'll be there. If for no other reason than to make sure

Zak behaves himself. The last thing we need right now is our lead going off the rails."

With that I drove to my flat where I downed two bottles of O-neg to quench the thirst Stacey had set off inside me, and then I went in the shower and jerked off thinking of how she'd felt held tight against my body.

* * *

The warmth of the club was in stark contrast to the cool night air as I stepped inside *Sheol*. Walking towards the bar, I saw my bandmates were already there. Zak seemed antsy, hopping from foot to foot, and it wasn't in sync with the beat of the music playing.

"He's waiting for a meeting with Abaddon," Rex explained as I shrugged off my jacket and laid it across a bar stool. "And he wants someone to go with him. I've told him he's twenty-four and last time he showed us, had a fully working set of balls."

"I'll go with you," I told Zak.

He leapt up and hugged me. "Thanks, Noah. I knew I could count on you." He side-eyed Rex.

"And with that, I'm going to get another beer and then I'm going to go looking for some pussy, rather than spend my time with this pussy." Rex pointed at Zak.

A tall man dressed in a suit approached us. "Abaddon will see you now." The guy, who was called Aaron, had taken the whole *Men in Black* image a little too far, with his suit, tie, and shades, bearing in mind we were in a dark basement club in the centre of London. He'd knocked into two chairs on his way over.

"Thanks, Aaron." We set off walking behind him. "Now keep your cool, Zak, or you'll get nowhere. Let me handle it."

"I'm fine. I know how I'm going to play it. I just need you there because Abaddon tries to trick me all the time."

"He is a demon," I reminded him.

Getting in the lift, we went down six floors, coming out into a dimension hardly anyone in London knew existed beneath the ground: the seventh hierarchy where the demon Abaddon ruled. Zak had traded his soul as a randy eighteen-year-old virgin as well as agreeing to keep supplying Abaddon with a quota of other souls. In return, Zak had become an incubi. At eighteen he hadn't thought he'd get bored of unlimited sex.

At twenty-four while trying to become a rock god it was a whole different matter.

We followed Aaron into Abaddon's office where he sat behind his desk gesturing to the two seats in front of him. "I'd say it's good to see you, Zak, but given it's only the beginning of the month, I'm inclined to think there's a problem?"

In his actual form, Abaddon looked like a bright-red,

ulcer-festooned slug. In front of us now, he was mistaken a lot for Brendon Urie.

"I have great news, Boss," Zak started. Inside, I groaned.

Abaddon—or Don as he called himself because his real name was a mouthful—sat back, crossing his arms over his chest, a bemused smirk curling the corner of his mouth.

"You do? Fabulous, let's hear it."

"We made the finals of Britain's Best New Band, and do you know what that means?" Zak ploughed on even though I could clearly see he was on a one-way trip to Loserville.

"I don't. Tell me." Don wiggled a brow.

"It means that every week we progress, more women are hanging around us. If we reach the final, there are going to be so many willing women whose souls I can plunder. So... I thought maybe you'd agree I need to concentrate on my music and then do a double whammy next month...?"

Don stared at Zak and time seemed to stand still. Then he threw his mug from his table which just missed the top of Zak's head before smashing into the wall behind with such force it created a hole. He'd deliberately missed and that was to show Zak how close to losing his own head he was.

"Nope. But it is fabulous news. You can get this

month's quota as normal and then next month bring me more and I might let you have Christmas week off."

"I should get holiday entitlement anyway," Zak mumbled under his breath.

"I'm the leader of the seventh hierarchy. My name means The Destroyer," Don reminded Zak for what was no doubt the billionth time. "You will bring me part of the souls of satiated women as we agreed. You get your part of the bargain do you not?"

"Yes, Boss."

"Is there anything else?"

"No," Zak said sullenly.

It was my turn to try. "Zak's falling asleep all the time which means our chances of winning go down considerably, which means his chances of going down could also reduce considerably if you get my drift," I told Don. "He doesn't usually make much sense, but if he does have less to do now it would help the band. I think we have a pretty good chance of reaching the finals. We're 3:1 at the bookmakers right now and the press stuff is looking good."

Don tapped his fingers on his desk and his gaze went to the side for a moment, before returning to me. "I'll reduce his quota by half in October. In November I expect triple numbers, whether he's through to the final or not. Deal or no deal?" Don guffawed. "I always wanted to say that. Where's a red box when you need one?"

"There'll be plenty of red boxes if Zak has to satisfy triple the number of women in November," I quipped.

Don laughed again. "Oh, Noah, you are such fun, and of course I can't touch you seeing as you have no soul anyway, so you are as close to a friend as a demon can have. Great to touch base. Zak, cat got your tongue?" Don turned to me. "The pussy will have it soon, right?"

I laughed back.

Zak pouted. "Deal." He held out his hand. Don shook it and there was a loud bang and a sizzle, along with the smell of burned flesh, although when Zak removed his hand there was no damage or burn marks.

"Good luck with the contest. Tell the other two I said hi," Don said. Then he turned to Aaron, who'd been standing in the corner like a statue. "Well, go and bring my mug back, Aaron, or get me a new one if I broke it, and a fresh hot cup of tea. Do I have to remind you of your job?"

"No, Boss," Aaron said. "I'll show these two to the lift and then I'm on it."

"PG Tips. I can tell when you're pissed at me and try to sneak an own brand in. My poker has a very red-hot tip you know?" Don yelled at him, then he winked at me. "I don't get off on it sexually, but from a pain point of view, it's exquisite."

Yep, it was definitely time to leave, before Zak pissed his pants in fear.

***

On our way back up in the lift, Zak kept huffing and puffing.

"What the fuck is wrong with you? You just got your workload cut in half. Celebrate. Be happy."

"Why does he take no notice of me, but is all pally-pally with you?"

"He said why. I have no soul. He deals in them. I'm of no use to him so he may as well be friends with me. I'm sure if he found a way to screw me over, he would."

A voice came out from the top corner of the lift. "Yep, I would. Sorry, pal."

Zak jumped. "You have the lift bugged?" he spoke to the lift walls.

"I'm a demon. I have everything bugged. Zak, you really are going to have to wise up when it comes to demonology."

"Like I have time to study anything except the female body," Zak whined.

I gave him a dirty look. "It's not going to get you much sympathy, that line, mate."

"It sounds a lot better than it is. Trust me."

Having stepped out of the lift, we re-joined our bandmates. Rex was back and I caught him licking the back of his hand.

"Stop preening."

"I'm happy. I just got some in the ladies bathroom."

Roman, as usual, was drunk as a skunk. Two women came up to him and whispered in his ear. "I'm off to dance," he told us, before heading towards the floor, an arm through each female's folded one.

"Let's go dance too," Zak yelled over the music. "Because tonight I don't have to satisfy a woman and take her soul. I'm having the night off."

"You do realise we have the first live round tomorrow, don't you?" I pointed out. Sometimes I felt like their father.

"It's eleven o'clock. I promise to be in bed by midnight." Zak crossed his heart. "And for once I can categorically state it will be my own. I can't wait. Proper rest. A full night's sleep." He stood still for a moment thinking.

"Night guys," he said and with that he left.

I shook my head at Rex. "Let's get another drink, keep an eye on Roman, and make sure we're out of here by twelve. Tomorrow's a big day."

"Agreed. I'm off to get a pint. You having one?"

I shook my head, looking at one of the women Roman was dancing with. "Not a pint, more a quick shot."

Chapter Seventeen

THE DAILY NEWS

FRONT PAGE EXCLUSIVE

THE H-EX FACTOR

3 October 2022

As tonight's first live rounds get under way, we can reveal that The Paranormal's bass guitarist, Noah Granger, was the childhood sweetheart of Seven Sister's Stacey Williams.

A source close to them said, "They dated for a year in school, but then Noah ditched Stacey to form the other band and pursue his musical dreams."

Suddenly, it seems there might be more to watch the live shows for than just the music. Especially when Stacey has recently been seen in the company of Drayton Beyer, lead singer of Flame-Grilled Steak.

Chapter Eighteen
STACEY

We were backstage and waiting to go on stage for the first live show. With twenty acts, there were ten on a show today and ten tomorrow (a scandal had meant one of Carmela's other bands had been disqualified so all judges had an even amount of contestants again). Both my band and The Paranormals were appearing tonight. Drayton's Flame-Grilled Steak were on tomorrow night's show. Drayton had sent a bouquet of flowers to me. The note with them was as endearing as I figured he was going to get.

> Stacey,
>
> Good luck. I hope with all my heart your band are the runners up in the competi-

tion. But you're getting my D when this is all over, so you're a winner anyway!

Dray xo

Who said romance was dead?

The press were having a field day over my past relationship history with Noah, and Donna was fucked off with me for not having told her about him. The more time that passed, the more I wondered why I'd entered this competition at all. I'd been leaving rehearsals to find press hanging around the doors asking me if I was enjoying a threesome. I kept with my stock answer of I 'preferred a sevensome'.

Tonight's mixture of bands appeared to be human apart from us and The Paranormals. It was a live audience and after an emcee had been on stage to warm them up and tell them the do's and dont's of the evening, the judges came out to whoops and hollers from the studio audience before taking their seats. Carmela and Marianne were wearing outfits to try to outdo one another in terms of flashing the flesh and shock value, but they may as well have not bothered. Harley went out on stage to a loud chorus of applause far louder than theirs, and as the cameras flashed to the audience, I noticed a tightness around both of their mouths that no amount of Botox or fillers could disguise.

Harley faced the cameras.

"Hello and welcome to the first live final of Britain's Best New Band. Before we carry on with the competition, I would just like to take a moment to bring everyone's attention to the man who should be standing here tonight by my side."

The audience went quiet as a picture of Dan flashed up on the screen behind, along with a telephone number.

"As you know, our friend and colleague Dan is still missing. Dan, if you're watching, our thoughts are with you. Please get in touch and let someone know you're okay. Our best regards go out to Dan's family, and if anyone at home has any information on his whereabouts, then please ring this number that goes to the team working on locating him. Thank you."

Marianne stood up. "Dan was the best fucking presenter ever." She kind of fell back in her seat and then looked around at the others, a dazed expression on her face.

Harley smiled. "Indeed, he *is* a fantastic presenter. On behalf of the show and to anyone offended by the use of language, I apologise."

"What the hell just happened then?" Kiki said to the rest of us.

"Looks like Marianne's had too many uppers before she came out." Shonna laughed.

The cameras went back to Harley. "Our first band

tonight are on Team Bill. So, Bill, would you like to introduce your band and tell us a little about their song tonight?"

The camera panned in on Bill. "My first band on stage tonight are called The Paranormals." There was a cheer from the crowd. "These four guys definitely have what it takes to go the whole way through this competition. Tonight's song choice shows the lead, Zak's, vocal talents in all their glory. They will be singing *Toxic* by Britney Spears."

"You heard it from Bill. Tonight's first act, singing *Toxic*, is The Paranormals." Harley held up a hand to the side of the stage and the band walked on stage while she walked off.

When the live shows happened, everyone got a makeover. From the lame looking act that had gone through the auditions, Noah's band had now been primped and preened to perfection. Zak's hair was short, dyed platinum blonde, and hair paste had been used to create a spiked effect. He was dressed in tight, black leather trousers that left nothing to the imagination, along with a white vest top. It showed off his muscled arms, and the tattoo of a death eater on the top of his right bicep.

Rex had taken to the drums at the back, his large body like a shadow of a boulder. Just his head and massive corded arms visible. His hair had been cut into his neck, but curls hung over one side of his face.

Roman wore tight silver jeans, a baggy black t-shirt with Alice Cooper on the front and the word Poison across it, and he had silver jewellery that ran from his ear to a nose stud. Against his dusky skin he looked electric, and I loved the poison/toxic connotations that wardrobe had put in. Like as if they were saying, *warning: this band can get in your bloodstream.*

Noah certainly seemed in mine.

I finally allowed my eyes to rest on him as he took his place and began to strum the guitar. All I could think of was those digits on my body instead. His dark hair was spiked like Zak's, but buzz cut below, rather than short. They'd put him in faded blue jeans that hugged his thighs, and a black short-sleeved shirt open at the neck. His chain hung down with the plectrum on it between the sides of his collar, taking me back to seeing him walk past me and ignore me when we were young. It still hurt. I wished with all my heart it didn't, but he still made me feel things I should have got over by now.

As their performance began, every one of them lit up like they'd been plugged into Blackpool illuminations, especially Noah. His dark eyes seemed to spark under the lights, the music seeping into his very being, and I realised that it would be wrong to separate this man from his music. So very wrong. Because although Noah was to all intents and purposes dead, with music he became very much alive.

It hit me then that Noah was married to his music. He'd made that commitment long ago, in the days when he'd left me behind. Some part of me now understood as I watched him work the crowd, giving them a cheeky smirk. Not because he was flirting with them, but because he was so happy to be standing where he was.

I had an amazing vocal. I knew that. And my band were good. But I also knew that next to The Paranormals, at this moment we weren't going to win. Because you had to give it your all up there, and some of me still belonged to the man on stage.

The audience went insane as the band finished their number. The judges went wild in their feedback, with Bill becoming increasingly smug.

Harley went to join the band on stage. "Wow, The Paranormals. What a first performance. What do you think to the judge's feedback... Zak?"

Zak stroked a fingertip across his eyebrow. "We are truly honoured." He did a thank you, clutching his chest. "It's a privilege to be on this stage performing in front of so many people."

"And, Roman?" Roman looked shocked that she chose him to speak to, although I knew why. "You seem to be the quietest member of the band. Is that true or are you a dark horse?"

"Wrong animal, right, kid?" Zak sniggered, and Harley looked at him with a creased brow.

Roman leaned closer to the microphone. "It's hard to get a word in edgeways with Zak here, but I'm so happy to be in the band, and thank you to all the judges. We hope we'll be able to entertain you all again next week."

With that they made their way off stage.

We were the closing act and so I didn't know what possessed me, but I decided to go through to their dressing room and congratulate them on their performance. The corridor was busy, and I could see people going in and out, but I carried on, walking forward, and pushing open the door.

To find the dark-haired woman with her arms wrapped around Noah. She was kissing him in a frenzy, dotting kisses all over his face and then she held his face in her hands.

"My baby. They've made you look even more handsome. You looked so good out there."

I knew what he'd said to me about Mya being the one who made him a vampire and that there'd never been a romance, but I saw a bond between them that hurt my head and heart so bad I felt like I'd been spiked through my own. I staggered back and away before he saw me and returned to our own dressing room.

"Where'd you disappear off to?" Donna asked.

"Just needed a quick walk. I'm feeling nervous." It was only a half-lie.

"Well, no more disappearing now, because we don't

want to have to invoke my mediumship skills again to locate you." She laughed.

Donna had been unable to turn up any more information on either Dan or Jack and had just dropped the matter as if she'd spent the other evening colouring in a picture and then scrunched it up and thrown it in the bin. I didn't know how she could be okay being possessed by a dead person's spirit one day and then act like it had never happened the next. She was a peculiar one was our Donna. After her outburst the other day, I was trying to make sure I listened to her and didn't overlook her because of her being small. She'd been right to call me out on it and I actually felt a little ashamed of my behaviour.

That was why I'd decided that she should provide the main backing vocals tonight and be a bit more visible on stage.

We sang Britney's *Womanizer* and I put all my internalised anger into the song to such a point that to my utter amazement we received a standing ovation.

"Fucking hell, Stacey, where did that come from?" Estelle tapped me on the shoulder. "Even I'm turned on and I'm dead inside according to my husband." She turned to the others. "If she keeps this up, we're winning this thing."

I saw that Donna's expression looked sullen. "There's credit due to Donna too," I said. "I think her backing vocals made me sound better than I was."

"Yeah, I think so too. I think I added a harmonic element that made your performance seem to zing," Donna claimed.

Ultimately, I didn't give a shit. I was really beginning to wonder why I was even there. The more this competition progressed, the less it seemed about being connected with my dreams and the more it seemed to be about settling a score with an ex.

There was no doubt that I loved singing. I loved my friends and coven sisters, and singing in the band had given me the same sense of belonging I'd had when I sang with Noah. But was that it? Was the family/friend/support part of it the main reason I did it? If someone said to me right now, 'Go solo and we'll give you a recording contract', would I? Did I want it as a career? Did I really want to win this competition and go on tour?

Fuck me. I didn't.

Looking around at my bandmates, I felt like I'd let them all down. Because I knew that I would do my best to win this competition for them, and then I was going to leave the band.

Stacey Williams wanted more. I wanted to be someone's everything. Not a lead singer. Not an ex. When I found someone who put me first above everything, I knew I'd follow that person to the ends of the earth.

Because all I'd ever been searching for was love.

* * *

Ten years earlier

"For God's sake, Stacey, get out from under my feet, and stop making that noise," my mum yelled at me for the billionth time that day. She'd been telling me all my life I'd been a mistake, and as soon as I was old enough to look after myself, she went out with her mates and largely ignored me. Oh, she made sure there was always a pizza or a microwave curry in the fridge, and left me money for buying clothes, but she'd had me at fifteen, didn't talk to her parents—my grandparents—and said it was her time now.

I grabbed my schoolbag and set off to school early. I bought toast and a drink at breakfast club and then walked around the halls looking at the noticeboard, wasting time until the bell went. I didn't really have any friends. People knew I was from the Scarsdale Estate and so pretended I didn't exist because only the poor or those with mental illness lived there. Social housing prejudice at its finest.

I spotted the notice.

Choir
Singers required for school plays. Rehearsals

Monday and Fridays 4pm, more sessions nearer to performance dates.

It was perfect. I could sing without my mum harping on, and it kept me out of the way.

I'd been there about three months when Noah joined. I spotted him sitting at the back in the corner. He looked as lonely as I felt so I went over to him.

"Hi, I'm Stacey."

He stared up at me and my heart thudded a little because up close I saw how gorgeous his eyes were, with his long, dark lashes. "Noah," he replied.

"You don't look all that excited to be here." I sat beside him, and he didn't tell me to move which led me to think he was okay with it.

"Truth? I'm here because my enemies won't come here for me. It's not worth it, and hopefully they'll have got bored and left before I get out."

"So you don't actually want to be in the choir?" I said, disappointed.

"Oh I love music, and I'm happy enough to be here, although I didn't really need another excuse for them to call me gay or a pansy, but Mrs Hellier seems to think it'll help me with my 'issues'."

Mrs Hellier was the school pastoral counsellor.

"If it's any consolation, I'm here because my mother doesn't want me at home. I don't have any friends either. Not because I'm bullied, but because people like to pretend I don't exist."

Noah turned to me. "I don't know how anyone could not notice you. You're really pretty." Then he blushed. But that was the day I became friends with Noah Granger and a week later he asked if I wanted to be his girlfriend. The rejection from others meant we'd found each other.

And that was why Noah should have known more than anyone how his actions would affect me, when he rejected me later.

* * *

The results show wasn't until ten pm the following evening, so as tears threatened to overflow my lower lashes, I faked a yawn and turned to my friends.

"I'm totally beat, so I'm going to make tracks, okay? I'll see you all tomorrow."

I caught the Tube back to my house and sat with the curtains open while I stared at the moonlight. I was alone, but I felt a sense of peace I'd not had in a long time as I enjoyed my own company and own home. And as I sat on my sofa looking out, I realised where I was yet again going wrong. I wanted someone to love me.

Yet, I didn't love myself.

That was where I needed to start. To find out what made Stacey Williams happy inside. And work out what came after the end of this competition.

Getting out my candles, I created a spell of optimism, and for a few minutes it seemed to hang in the air like diamond dust. I slept better that night than I had in years.

Chapter Nineteen

NOAH

We came off stage on a natural high. There was just no feeling like it... well other than the time I'd sunk deep into Stacey after that concert, but I tried not to let my mind dwell on that. Our plans had been to shower, change, and go watch the rest of our competition, but it soon became apparent that I wasn't going to get to do that any time soon when the door pushed open and Mya walked in, accompanied by her husband, Death, a man who made Aaron the security guy look like a comedian.

Mya flung herself at me. "Surprise!"

"I'll say this is a surprise," I stated. "You didn't even give out a tiny tweak on the mind meld." I hugged her and she beamed at me.

"It wouldn't have been much of a surprise if I did that, would it?" She turned to everyone else. "You were all phenomenal out there. You'd better win. I've taken a bet on you."

"I hope you got it in early, because we're on evens at the moment," Roman informed her.

"Oh, sweetpea. I haven't bet like that. I've told a tormented soul he can have ten minutes with his ex if he doesn't win."

Roman backed away from Mya with haste, made his excuses and went to the showers.

"Hey, De—" I began to say, but Mya's husband scowled at me, reminding me that it probably wasn't a good idea to announce his name in public.

"De-nny," I said instead.

Mya burst into laughter. "Denny. Denny-wenny. Might call you that instead of Big D."

I pulled a grimace at Death. Yup my sire was wed to the Grim Reaper himself. "Sorry!"

He shrugged. "I'm used to her by now."

Rex walked over and held out his hand for Denny to shake, but Mya jumped over and slapped it down to his side.

"Don't do that. You'll feel like death," she told him.

Rex looked at me, quirked a brow, and made his excuses, saying he needed water.

Death's attention shot to the doorway. "There's a soul here. I'm confused though. It's unhappy and happy at the same time."

"Denny, darling. Can you shut up?" Mya scolded him. "I'm here to see my son, not to work."

Zak raised a brow. "If you were my sire, I'd have definite mummy issues".

Death stepped forward, "Pardon?"

"Nothing. Time for me to go shower." Zak departed with haste.

There was only Rex left in the room now, standing over at the drinks trolley. Rex had never felt threatened in Mya's company, not that they'd seen each other often. But vampires and shifters had a history, sometimes good, sometimes bad. A shifter would never show fear in front of a vamp and vice versa unless they really were in the shit.

"You know Denny and I have very busy careers, but I'll make sure I get to every live round where possible," Mya stated, "and I will definitely be at the final if you get through. I'm so proud of you. Your mum would be too."

"Oh sorry, did she pass? I can try to ask for permission for you to visit the Home of the Wayward as a one off. I can't promise though," Death said.

My brow creased. "No, she just moved to Australia. Met the love of her life. Lives off grid without any television. Surfs a lot and sends me the odd letter."

"Oh."

"I've told you that before. You men never listen," Mya scolded.

I'd been so happy for my mum when she'd met Matt.

I'd insisted she went and lived her best life. She'd done everything she could for me. I didn't want her to think she had to sacrifice anything more. Knowing she was happy made me happy. That was all I could ask for. My mother knew I was a vampire as I'd had to explain why I wasn't aging. She hadn't bought my excuse of a good face cream as she assured me she'd tried them all and 'None fucking worked, so you're lying, son'.

She'd then met Mya who had assured her she would take on a motherly role, being that she'd sired me anyway. It had all been bizarre and Mya had called me son ever since, which given she looked about three years older than me had garnered us some weird looks at times.

"My baby. They've made you look even more handsome. You looked so good out there." Mya started hugging me again and dotting me with kisses which she thought mums did. She held my face in her hands.

Then she dropped her hands and sniffed the air.

"So, are you and Stacey still on the outs?" she asked.

"Yep, you know that ship sailed a long time ago," I replied.

"Really? Only I just smelled her approach. Her blood is so damn sweet, but then it went away, so I'm guessing she changed her mind. Has her band been on yet?"

I groaned. My guess was that if Stacey had headed this way, she'd taken one look at Mya and turned on her heel.

"Seven Sisters are closing the show," I told her.

"Great, we'll stay and watch."

Death groaned. "I can only hope someone in the audience dies to get me out of here."

"But you love music," I queried.

"Music, yes. The hours taken to film a TV programme... let's just say Hell puts individuals in such scenarios as part of their torture rituals."

"Quit whining. Parents are supposed to be supportive." Mya turned towards me. "Okay, we'll leave you to shower. Catch you later." She gave me another hug.

Death gave me one of his smiles and a small wave. Even all these years later his rictus grin was enough to have a person running for the hills. But he tried, bless him, and that's what counted.

* * *

"Is it me, or does the audience seem particularly enraptured by every appearance Harley makes?" Zak asked me from the wings.

"They've all been told how to act, haven't they? They said on the live shows they'd let them be a bit more natural, but they all look like brainwashed zombies."

We looked at them when Harley was on stage, mouths open, especially the guys. The guys whose wives would think they had an amazing hubby because he'd helped their dreams come true by going to the Hex Factor live shows with them, when really, they were looking at Harley and the female judges and depositing material for the spank bank.

"You've got to admit, she's a great presenter. Not to knock Dan—he was good too—but she's better off when she's not sharing the stage."

Zak stumbled forward and then looked behind him.

"What's up with you? Had too much beer?" I asked.

"Someone just pushed me. I felt their hand on my back."

I turned and looked at the space around us. "Think you need to hit the sack, mate, because you're already dreaming."

He was about to protest, but then Seven Sisters came on stage. As Stacey not only captivated the audience but received a standing ovation from the crowd and the judges, we became otherwise occupied.

"Fuck, your ex might just be a thorn in our side in winning this competition. Do you reckon they're using their powers and bewitching everyone?" Roman asked.

"No, she wouldn't do that."

"It's clear we need to up our game, and I'd thought I was faultless, so actually you lot need to up your game," Zak chastised us. "We didn't get a standing ovation. You lot aren't working hard enough."

A security guy pulled back the curtain to where we were standing.

"You've got two reporters at the door to your dressing room. Got time to talk to them?"

"Do they want to talk to Seven Sisters or any of the other bands too?" Zak asked.

"Didn't say so. Just showed a press badge and asked for you." Security guy looked bored. It was nearly time to wrap things up and no doubt he was looking forward to going home.

"We're on our way," I told him, and we left the wings and went back to the dressing room.

* * *

What we found at our door didn't look much like press. It looked a lot more like two twenty-somethings, one of whom, a woman with pink hair, was so drunk she could barely stand. The drunk one took one look at Zak and blurted out, "Fuck me. I really do think I died."

I saw the other woman elbow her in the side.

Zak looked bored. "I'm off. You can sort out whatever this is," he whispered in my ear. Then he turned on the charm for the women, saying it was good to meet them, but he had an urgent appointment, and off he went. Twat.

The pink-haired one's drunk eyes followed him the whole way down and she let out a regretful sigh.

"Let's get you on your feet and some coffee down

you," I said, looking from one woman to the other. "And don't pretend to be press. I know you aren't."

I did have to hold in a snigger and eyeroll when the pink-haired one asked, "How?"

"I can read both your minds," I said honestly. "You couldn't be more open if you had a shop sign hung around your neck."

"It's you," the brunette huffed, side-eying her friend. "Being drunk gave the game away."

Inviting them into our dressing room, I asked their real names and discovered the brunette was Freya and 'pink' was called Erica.

Erica was still legless, but then her eyes widened, and she announced: "It's true I'm not a press person. I'm the president of your fan club."

"Fan club?" I smirked.

"Yes." Erica was becoming more exuberant as she warmed to her own idea which she was clearly thinking up as she went along. "Whether you win or not, I believe you are on the brink of stardom, and I want to run your official fan club. What say you?"

Rex shot forward, his hair flying around his face. "Hell, yeah. I even know what we can call our fans."

"Oh God, don't encourage him," Roman groaned.

"The Subs," Rex said proudly. "Do you get it? Short for subscribers to our club, but meaning submissive, doing what we want them to."

Freya's hand shot up. "I want to be the first official Sub."

He winked at her. "Done. So, coffee, and then you can take some notes about the band; how we started up etc. Sound good?" His voice had gone extra husky.

Freya took the notepad and pen from Erica. "While my bestie sobers up, I can start by getting to know you. Is there somewhere more comfortable we could go?"

Freya's mind was a cacophony of cuss words when both Rex and Roman suggested going to the canteen and it looked like she would actually have to write down some facts about the band. Seemed like I was staying with Erica and sobering her up.

* * *

"Will my friend currently be part of a threesome?" was the first thing Erica asked when more in control of her faculties.

I laughed. "No. She's quite safe in the canteen. You'll have just made their day by saying you're making a fan club. Don't worry, I'll let them down gently. Sorry that Zak left when I know you came to see him."

"Was I that obvious?" Erica said, her mouth turning down at the corners.

I didn't want to say I could read her mind again, so I smiled gently. "A little."

"Huh. Yeah, he was so interested, he left in a split-second."

I patted her arm. "Zak has a great amount on his plate, not least of which is we're trying to win this competition. I definitely wouldn't pin your hopes on him. He's not a settling down kind of guy. Or a one-woman kind of guy." I hoped she wouldn't start crying, but she was on a one-way ticket to brokenheartsville if she pursued Zak.

"Is Stacey really with Dray? Because I think you two look good together."

I'd not expected that one. She bloody could be press; the woman had a natural flair for asking you questions you felt you wanted to answer. "Matchmaker, are you?"

"You must be joking. I can't get myself a date, never mind anyone else. Nope, if you still like Stacey you're on your own there. I just think you seem nicer than Dray."

I smirked. "But you don't actually know me. What if I'm a vampire or something and not as nice as you think?"

She guffawed with laughter. "I like you, you're stupid." Clapping her hand over her mouth, she gasped. "Sorry, I mean, you're funny, not stupid as in a fool. You make me laugh. I don't laugh much. My life's pretty boring, so I'm so pleased I'm now running your fan club." She patted down her pockets. "Oh, but Freya went off with my pad and pen so I can't write down anything you tell me."

"It's fine. You don't have to run our fan club. I'll tell

the others. Thanks for supporting us, and hopefully, you now realise that alcohol is not your friend."

She blushed a little. "I shouldn't let myself get pulled into Freya's hairbrained ideas, but hey, I got to meet you all. And I really am a huge fan and would definitely, truly, like to run your fan club. You'll need one. You're going to be huge. I just know it."

Oh, what the hell. "Give me your phone number and email address and we'll be in touch. You can totally run our fan club if you want. You can ask us anything via emails and then we'll leave how you run things up to you. That's if you wake up in the morning still wanting to be our fan club president and it's not the alcohol talking."

"I don't usually drink," she confessed.

"Funnily enough, I kind of worked that out." I stood up and escorted her to the door. "Let's go find your friend in the canteen."

She nodded.

"I really do think you and Stacey seem better suited than her and Dray," she said, as her friend stood up in the canteen and they got ready to leave.

"You stick to creating the fan club, and I'll run my love life, or lack of it." I gave her a hug.

"Bye. It was nice to meet you. Thanks for being so kind and not kicking us out," Erica said.

Bless her. Erica seemed a really nice girl. I hoped she wasn't taking on this fan club thing just to try to get near

Zak. Her soul seemed far too good for him. He'd ruin her. But... she was a grown woman, and I clearly had no clue about love, so it wasn't my problem.

We said goodbye to the women and made our way home.

* * *

Back at the show the following evening, we found we'd made it through to the following week's live rounds. So had Seven Sisters and Flame-Grilled Steak.

Chapter Twenty
STACEY

For someone who seemingly had the world at her feet if the stories in the press were anything to go by, I was pretty damn miserable. I'd enjoyed my time alone, but now I was back here waiting for the results to be announced and the amount of people and noise surrounding me was overwhelming.

Most of the chatter was coming from my bandmates as Donna almost had them in a frenzy with her excited chatter about how we could win this. She was full of ideas about what we could do next, and I noticed Carmela smiled at her without it reaching her eyes. We did what Carmela told us, end of. She'd been okay with the changes we'd suggested last time, but as she cast her eyes upon Donna once more, I got the impression that the already small Donna was going to get cut down soon.

I only wished I had the same enthusiasm.

We walked out onto the stage for the bit where there was the overexaggerated announcement of who had and hadn't made it to the next round. For the first week we were being whittled from twenty acts to seventeen acts and then two acts a week would leave for the next seven weeks, leaving three acts in the final.

* * *

We made it through to the next week. I was happy for the band, but I still had this unsettled feeling inside. After making my excuses to be on my own for a second night in a row, I went home where I took some time trying to work out what was making me feel this way. Okay, I'd realised I needed to focus on myself a little, but that couldn't be it. I had this edgy feeling, and thinking about it, I'd had it since Donna had done her contacting of the dead.

I needed answers. She'd supposedly had Jack Brooks talking through her. I wanted to know if Noah had killed him. He'd acted like he was unaware that Jack had taken my virginity, but he'd been around at that time. He could have been following me.

Taking out my grimoire, I laid it open on a blank page. After crushing sage on it, I dusted the sage off into my wastepaper bin and then I threw down some black soot on the white paper. I recited my spell.

"Goddess, I have cleared the page.
And now I've made a mess.
Please come forward to my aid,
And form in an address."

I carried on. "Please tell me the address for Noah Granger, my ex-boyfriend." The soot re-arranged itself, forming a London address, and then the soot soaked into the page, leaving a black written imprint. I thanked the goddess, noted the address, and ordered an Uber.

* * *

It was clear Noah wasn't expecting to see me. Thinking about it, he hadn't been forced to be home, but luckily, he was. He rubbed his eyes. "Sorry, Stace. I wasn't expecting you, was I...?" He looked tired. A rare look on a vampire.

"No, you weren't. I wasn't expecting to be here either. Can I come in?" I waited a few seconds.

Noah nodded his head. "Yeah, course you can. Sorry, I just need a minute to wake up. I'd nodded off on the sofa. All this rehearsing is making me need a bit more sleep than usual. Come through and make yourself at home while I go throw some water on my face, and then I'll put the kettle on." He paused. "Unless you want something stronger?"

"A coffee would be good. Thanks."

I walked inside. Noah's place wasn't a million miles away from my own studio apartment. We'd both gone for no-frills, 'places to rest your head' décor, and I wondered if it meant that like me, he'd not found anywhere he felt he could call home yet.

After asking how I drank my coffee, he brought two mugs in and placed them on top of a music magazine lying on the coffee table in front of the sofa. I'd taken a seat on the sofa and so Noah sat in the nearby chair.

"Okay, so let's cut to the chase now. Why are you here, Stace?"

I took a deep breath. "Did you murder Jack Brooks?"

"That's why you came here?" Noah jumped up and started pacing, scrubbing a hand through his hair. As he turned to me, a tic pulsed in his cheek. "You think I'm capable of that?" He walked over to his window, pulling back the curtains and staring out into the night sky.

"You had yourself turned into a vampire. I don't know what you're capable of," I said truthfully.

Noah sucked in his top lip for a moment. "No, I didn't kill Jack Brooks. That's the truth, but you can choose to believe it or not, seeing as you don't know what I'm capable of." He threw my words back in my face.

"And I know he's missing, but are you saying they've found a body?"

"No." I looked up at him. "Please sit down, Noah. I need to talk about this with someone, and you'll understand, being supernatural."

Slowly, he wandered back over, but this time he sat beside me on the sofa. "What's going on?"

I sighed. "My friend and bandmate Donna decided to do some mediumship and she claimed to be possessed by Jack. He'd become furious and said it was my fault he was dead. Then she was sick, and he 'left'." I air quoted left.

"And do you trust this Donna? Know that she wasn't winding you up in some way?"

"Yes, I'd trust her with my life. We've been friends for a long time. She's a coven sister. She's just guilty of being a little impulsive. But that's what was said, and with your history, I'd always wondered..."

"If I'd returned and drained him in a revenge plot for everything he'd done to me?" Noah stated.

"Well, yes."

"Stacey, Jack was a dickhead who made my life a misery. A bully. But the worst thing he did to me was name-call me and give me a kicking. Not things that in my book equate with me taking his life. It crossed my mind to give him a good kicking back at first, given I was a hell of a lot stronger, but I couldn't be bothered. Once I'd been turned, I had no interest in losers like Jack Brooks, who made themselves feel better by picking on others."

"And loser girlfriends," the words were out before I could stop them.

"No," Noah said vehemently. "I'll keep saying this over and over again until the day someone puts a stake through my heart. I let you go because I was a danger to you. Have you any idea how your sweet, virginal blood sang to me? As a newly turned vampire I would have fucked you raw and then drained you dry, Stacey. I'm not lying. You were in complete and utter danger from me. I had to feed myself on bottles of blood to the point of wanting to be sick in case I caught a passing glimpse of you. Rex was my main wingman, because as a shifter he could hold me down if it looked like I might bolt towards you."

"But you hardly ever looked my way."

"Stace, I didn't need to. I could smell you from miles away. I daren't look because if I had, I was afraid that Rex wouldn't have been able to hold me down. You weren't a witch then, or maybe, you'd just started hanging around them, I don't know; but you certainly wouldn't have been any match for me. It's been hard enough trying to exist without you in my life. But it's been a hell of a lot better than being responsible for your death, because make no mistake, I. Would. Have. Killed. You."

"I-it's been hard trying to exist...?" I repeated what I was sure he'd just said.

"Very hard. In more ways than one." His eyes hooded as he stared at me hungrily. "You'd better leave now, Stacey, if I've satisfied what you came here for." There was no mistaking the implication in his tone or his expression.

"You have, but now I have another question," I told him.

He sighed. "Yes?"

"Do you still want to fuck me raw?" I asked.

His answer was that his eyes flashed red, his fangs descended, and he pulled me into his arms and through to his bedroom at a speed that made me dizzy.

* * *

His bedroom was shades of grey, shadowed by the half-closed curtains at the window. He threw me down onto the top of his duvet and I bounced slightly. Scooting up the top of the bed and resting my back against the pillows, I looked up as Noah stood against the end of the bed.

"You'll have to promise me you're not going to just slip out in the middle of the night this time, Stacey."

"Why? I have a home. Why would I not go to it afterwards?" I retorted.

"Because you belong in my arms and if you can't stay there forever, at least stay there this one night."

I nodded. My body was overridden with lust, and I'd worry about the fallout once I'd had a few orgasms.

Noah stripped off his clothes and my mouth went so dry I had to lick around my lips. He was lean but sculpted, his arms threaded with corded muscle. A dark trail of hair ran down from his belly button to his groin where his hard cock rose in a greeting. He grasped his length and pumped it a few times. I grasped the bottom of my sweater ready to lift it up, and then he was there, kneeling astride me, helping me.

His gaze grazed over me hungrily as he feasted on the sight of me in just my red lacy bra and panties. Pulling down a cup, his tongue flicked over my already hard nipple and then he nipped softly. I looked down to see if he'd drawn blood—he was a vampire with a cracking set of incisors after all—but no. He gave the same attention to my other nipple and then he ripped the fabric of my bra in half.

"Noah! I could have magicked it off. Now you've ripped it."

He grinned, his eyes flashing with mischief. "I always wanted to do that. You can magic yourself a replacement pair, because..." He ripped my panties clean off me. Then he moved down between my legs, and I stopped giving a crap about my undies being torn.

I didn't want to think about where he'd practised this stuff to such a professional level. It had been three years since we'd fucked and he'd got even better, damn him. But then I was no virgin either. We both had pasts.

Shut up, Stacey. You're shagging Noah and your brain is going on and on when this amazing lover is between your legs.

Fair point, I told myself and concentrated on what he was doing again.

That talented tongue delved in and out of me and tickled at my nub until it teased me to the point of no return. As I began to convulse against his mouth, I grabbed Noah's hair and rode his face until my body sagged with satisfaction. I felt like I'd had a truckload of Valium or something I was that chilled out. And then Noah bit the top of my thigh. My blood fizzed and whirled as it responded to his vampire touch. His venom captivated my cells, leading them into a dance where I felt like they almost did a conga all the way into Noah's mouth. My core clenched and I raised my thighs as he sucked on me.

Breaking off, Noah moved so he was above me and he knelt between my thighs guiding his cock to where my soaking wet pussy was waiting.

As Noah pushed inside me, I gasped in sheer and utter pleasure and wrapped my legs around him.

"God, you feel so fucking good, Stace," he groaned as he moved in and out of me.

All I could do was moan my clear agreement.

Noah grabbed my breast and tweaked a nipple as he continued to thrust, and then he moved his hand to between us, flicking my clit while he changed to lazy strokes. I opened my eyes because I could sense his gaze on me.

"What?"

"You're just so fucking beautiful," he said. "And so fucking *mine*."

And as if he knew I'd protest against his words, he chose that moment to bite my neck and slam against me in a hard thrust. Then I was spinning and lost in a vortex of ecstasy as my mind, body, and soul exploded in satisfaction.

Panting against Noah, I slowly came back down to earth. He licked at my neck, and I knew from our last encounter that he was sealing the bite wounds.

"Say nothing if you can't say anything good." He smirked, looking down at me.

"That was amazing," I told him. "I'm definitely staying the night."

* * *

And I did. I slept in between bouts of bedroom antics and when I finally fell into a deep sleep at around four am, I knew nothing more until Noah woke me.

At midday.

"Shit!" I shot up and immediately went dizzy.

I scowled at Noah. "Is that because you bit me? Did you take too much?"

All I got in return was a bemused smirk. "No, Stacey. I hardly took a drop. It's because we screwed all night and you've just shot up quick."

"Oh."

"I wouldn't drain you."

"Such a romantic statement."

He tilted his head at me. "Do you want me to be romantic? I can be."

I rubbed at my eyes. "All I know right now is I want a cup of coffee. As for anything else, I seriously have no idea. I wasn't expecting this to happen."

"So you're not ready for my 'What does this mean' question?"

"God, you're a needy bitch." I laughed.

I couldn't really magic myself a new pair of undies, so I just had to put my top, sweater, and jeans back on. "Am I okay to grab a shower?" I asked.

"Sure. I'll be fixing that coffee. Is toast okay? I don't keep a lot in with not needing to eat."

"Yeah, that's fine."

I took my time in the shower thinking about what had happened between us. It didn't help that our bodies had melded perfectly together. But the fact remained that nothing had changed between us. He still put the band first and I was actually dating another guy. Okay, I'd not slept with Dray, but still, this hadn't been a cool thing to do. I wasn't that kind of woman who strung a guy along or kept things open. I know Dray flirted with other women, but that didn't mean that I should change my own stance on things.

Sitting at his kitchen island on a tall stool, Noah passed me a coffee. "I don't need to read your mind, you know," he told me. "Your truths are written all over your face."

I took a sip, scalding my tongue. "Could you put me a splash of cold in? I'm so thirsty."

"Me too." Noah winked.

My breasts and core perked up in response. Luckily, my brain was in situ this morning and leading the way forward.

"Noah..."

"I know. Nothing's changed," he replied, and then he looked up at me sharply.

"What if I did, Stacey? What if I quit right now, and left it all behind?"

"Pardon?" I was hearing things.

"What if I went back to the guys now and quit? Would you give us a chance?"

I wanted to say yes. I really did. But it was the wrong time and the wrong place again for us. I'd seen him on stage. It was in his blood. He would not be happy at a life without music. And I wasn't ready to give myself over to anyone right now. I needed to find my own path. Find out what I wanted to do after the competition.

"Oh," was all he said.

"I'm not saying we can never happen, Noah. But I don't want this right now. Us. It's not the right time for me." I got up off my stool. "Thanks for the coffee."

He nodded and then I walked out of the door, calling for an Uber to take me home from the street outside his place.

I felt like I'd just made a huge mistake. But was it sleeping with Noah, or walking away from him?

Chapter Twenty-One

NOAH

I threw myself into rehearsing for the live performances because it took my mind off Stacey. When I saw her, she'd smile at me like you would a friend, but she continued to hang around with Drayton. Looked like she'd made her choice. Why had she left me with hope, saying never say never? It twisted me up worse than being in the vicinity of kebab sticks.

"Look at this." Zak beckoned me over to look at his phone. "There's a piece in today's *Daily Mirror* about one of those women that said they were press. Apparently, she has set up a fan club with a newsletter and it's got fifteen thousand subscribers in two days."

I took the phone off him and sure enough there was a picture of Erica holding up a press photograph of us.

"Bill says he's getting his PA onto it and that he'll make sure that Erica lets us see what she's posting before she posts it, and in return he'll cover her costs and send her merch, tickets, etc. We might have to answer some inane questions he says, but it's all PR."

"She seemed a really nice woman," I said.

"Bloody naïve, she was, thinking she could hoodwink us into believing she was press."

"They got backstage and all the way to our dressing room," I reminded him.

"Yeah, well, security leaves a lot to be desired here, let's face it. I mean the fucking presenter disappeared."

"I wonder what did happen to him?" I pondered out loud.

"I dunno. Maybe Harley being a better presenter got to him and he's crying in a corner somewhere?"

Then Zak screamed, "Ow," and smacked at his arm.

"What?"

"Something nipped me hard. Or maybe it was a sting. It was bloody weird."

"Maybe Dan's dead and it was his ghost punishing you for your stinging comments. Get it? Stinging," I joked. "Anyway, it wasn't that long ago we were crying in corners, Zachariah. Remember where you came from."

"God, do you have to remind me? Though I believe I'm between a rock and a hard place, and by that, I mean I used to have rocks thrown at me at school, and now I'm constantly having to be hard."

"Look, you have a reprieve from Don and then after

the competition we'll have a think about your next options."

"There won't be any. I need to face facts. I made a deal with a demon and I'm going to have more access to souls than ever."

"The thing with demons is they get greedy and they like deals. We just have to find something that tempts him more than you. But right now, let's concentrate on rehearsing, okay?"

"Yes, Boss," he said, but he didn't look convinced.

* * *

The next few weeks were a constant merry-go-round of rehearsing, eating, and sleeping. Then the semi-finals approached. There were four bands left: us; Seven Sisters; Flame-Grilled Steak; and RokUrWorld, a human act with a singer, a cello player, and a synth player. They were all male and worked an EMO style. Being Irish and looking like they should be the lead in teen movies meant that they'd received a solid vote week after week from their country and from teenage girls.

My life had become nothing more than music, as once again I pushed my feelings about Stacey down somewhere deep inside myself and threw everything into the band. If I walked into the canteen and saw her with Dray, I'd nod at them as if I didn't give a toss and then ignore them and concentrate on my friends. I kept my desires satisfied by working my way through the female staff on the show. I was feeding off their blood and then Zak was appearing in some of their dreams at night to take a piece of their souls.

For this reason, there were rumours of a virus going around the catering staff and runners. As they were almost all female, no one had noticed that the male staff population were largely unaffected. Yup, sometimes one had flirted with Stacey, and being pathetic, I'd bit them and made them too tired to flirt any more. I wasn't proud of my behaviour, but well, bite me.

We had two tracks to perform for the show and Bill was taking a keen interest now in our performances. He'd made us change one song this week which put additional pressure on us to learn our altered performance quickly.

The pressure could be witnessed now as the atmosphere in the canteen during breaks was no longer frivolous. There was an underlying tension, and it was as if there was a rope being pulled tighter and tighter, ready to snap at any point.

And people were acting weirder.

Harley stood in the queue for food behind Dray, who stood behind Stacey. I was standing behind Harley.

Dray turned around to Harley beaming widely, while rubbing his right arse cheek.

"Hey, hey, hey, Harley Davies. Keep your hands to yourself, cos my missus might get mad."

Harley looked at him like he was deranged. "What are you talking about?"

"You felt my arse several times. Wanna ride me, Harley?"

"No, I don't, and I didn't feel any part of you, and especially not your bum. That would be sexual harassment; a bit like what you're doing now asking me if I want to ride you. I suggest you quit this conversation unless you want throwing out of the competition."

Drayton stood up to his full height and growled. "Hey, lady. You clearly touched me. Let's not accuse me of something I'm not doing. I'm with this chick." He pointed to Stacey, who was looking around at the audience we now had from the rest of the canteen. Dray's inner bear was coming out as his voice boomed a deep bass that carried around the place.

"Harley didn't touch you, Drayton. I'd have seen it."

His head shot around fast, so he was glaring at me. "Really, dude? Because every time I look, your eyes seem to be on my missus."

"Drayton, lower your voice," Stacey hissed under her breath. She moved so she was next to Harley and rolled her eyes in Harley's direction.

Harley turned to me. "Thanks, because I really didn't touch him. He's far too alpha for my liking."

"No problem," I said, but my mind was starting to think about the weird shit happening lately. Zak being pushed forward, Marianne's weird outburst, Zak's feeling of being pinched, and now this. Something was going on, but what? With a missing presenter and these weird occurrences, we needed to keep our wits about us, because something wasn't quite right.

Chapter Twenty-Two

ERICA

From: TheSubsofTheParanormals@gmail.com
Date: 15 November 2022
Subject: THEY MADE THE FINAL!!! (Of course they did).

From the ONLY OFFICIAL fan group of The Paranormals.

OMG did you see this week's live show? Of course, you did, you're a Sub!!! That rendition of Wildest Dreams! Like Carmela said they certainly put the wild into their performance. Did you growl too?!!!

But it's next week now that we need to get prepared for. Get your dialling fingers at the ready so we can have our

Paranormals crowned as Britain's Best New Band. (I'm already having to fan myself).

Also, don't forget to send any questions you have for the band to me, so I can go meet them and put your questions to them.

Aren't I the luckiest woman in the world? Please don't hate me, someone has to get you the lowdown on our rock gods.

Until next week (eeek).

Erica xoxo

Chapter Twenty-Three

THE DAILY NEWS

LOVE FEUD AS THE PARANORMALS, SEVEN SISTERS, AND FLAME-GRILLED STEAK BATTLE IT OUT FOR THE TITLE OF BRITAIN'S BEST NEW BAND.

16 November 2022

Saturday night's final looks like being the mother of all showdowns as guitarist Noah Granger from The Paranormals faces ex-girlfriend Stacey Williams of Seven Sisters and her rumoured new lover Drayton Beyer from Flame-Grilled Steak.

If rumours of a bust-up in the canteen this week between the three are true, then maybe the competition isn't just about the record deal but also about winning Stacey's heart?

The bets are on The Paranormals winning the show, but the true winner seems to be presenter Harley Davies, who has just signed a million-pound deal to be the face of ITV. This follows her success fronting the show this year alone after previous co-presenter Dan Trent went missing shortly after the first show of the new series.

Chapter Twenty-Four

DAN

For God's sake. Harley was impenetrable. My hate for her grew stronger every day, and I, in turn, became stronger. I could take over Marianne of all people. Probably because she'd always been a hole to sink into if her rumoured antics in the swinging sixties were anything to go by.

Other than that, it was parlour tricks. Amusing ones, but still not enough for me to possess Harley. If I'd had a substantial body, it was at that point I would have smacked myself up the head.

Why was I trying to possess Harley?

I could aim for the top. I could possess the boss himself, Bill Traynor. He acted like he was the big guy, but in actual fact his minions did everything for him. Without everyone around him feeding his ego he was nothing.

I laughed even though no one could hear it.

Chapter Twenty-Five
STACEY

It was the final rehearsals and Carmela was working us hard. The band were getting fed up. All apart from Donna. She'd placed herself into deputy position and was like a cheerleader captain.

Tempers flared at the first refreshment break of the day when Kiki spoke up. "I'm starting to think that I don't actually want to be part of a touring band," she said, wringing her hands. "I don't want to upset anyone, but I'd rather tell you how I'm feeling now, rather than before we might win. I'm actually missing my husband."

"You mean you want us to quit? Now, as we've reached the final?" Donna spat out.

"No. Not at all. I just mean that if you win, I don't want to, well, erm, carry on. I'm just going to go home. You don't need to be seven sisters. Most bands only have four in them."

"Four sisters. Yeah, that's witchy sounding," Donna huffed.

"You're bitchy sounding right now." Kiki's defences rose.

"Hey, hey," I said, trying to calm things down. "Let's just focus on the final. We might not even win, so you're arguing about a record deal and tour we might not get anyway."

"But what if we do?" Donna folded her arms across her chest.

"Then we can strip down to whoever wants to be in the band and negotiate."

She huffed. "Don't be ridiculous. Bill would just drop us and sign the runners up." She stormed off.

Kiki's eyes were glassy. I put my hand over hers. "Kiki, I have mixed feelings too."

"And me," Shonna added. "I think I'd rather sit home reading than have to learn all these dances all the time. It gets a bit repetitive."

"Does anyone else think Donna's turned into a demanding diva?" Meryl queried.

A couple of the others agreed, and I sighed internally. My band was at war and no one's heart seemed to be in winning anymore, apart from Donna's.

"Look, we can't get this far and then give up. I see why she's so pissed off. We've been all for it and then right at the final hurdle we're all falling down. We are Seven Sisters and we can win this competition." I roused the others. "Just think of the opportunities winning could bring. It doesn't necessarily have to be a tour. Maybe we could get some sponsorship for designer clothes and things. Let's just carry on for now."

Kiki and Shonna didn't look convinced.

"I promise you that I have your back if you decide it goes no further than the end of this competition."

They nodded.

"Right, let me go and calm Donna down," I told them. "Then we can get back to rehearsing."

* * *

I found Donna sitting outside in the main hall. She looked like she was waiting to see the headteacher, all agitated and fidgety. I sat on a plastic chair beside her.

"What's going on, Donna?"

"I feel like I'm finally being seen by people, you know, and now they want to take that away from me."

"Oh, Donna." I pulled her towards me, my arm around her. "You can't make other people do your bidding just to make yourself feel better."

She shrugged off my hold. "It's okay for you. Mrs I'm-between-two-guys-and-I-get-all-the-press-coverage.

There's more to this band than you, but you wouldn't know it. I'm fed up of being invisible, Stacey. I want to be seen."

"What's got into you lately? You're all nasty and it's just not like you." I stood up. I didn't need to be insulted when I was trying to help someone. "Carry on and there will be no band to sing tonight. You're scaring them off," I warned. She ignored me and so I left her and went back to rehearsals. She didn't return for the rest of that day and then the following day she acted like it had never happened.

It was a sign of the price of fame and how it could go to people's heads. I was becoming increasingly onside with Kiki and Shonna's point of view. I liked the clubs—playing smaller, more intimate venues—and the idea of staying at that level appealed. But it was probably too late now. Like Donna said, I was becoming a household name thanks to the imaginary war the press were dreaming up across their pages.

There was no fight for my heart.

And that would become clear at the final.

When the guys went all out to win for themselves.

* * *

The day following Donna's outburst we had a spectator watching our rehearsals. Dray was sitting on a stool in the corner of the studio after finishing up with his own band. His eyes watched our every move. If I'd had a true interest in him, I'd be seriously pissed off that his attention wandered so much to the others, but my feelings didn't go beyond me liking him and enjoying his company. I knew I'd have ended our 'dating' by now if it wasn't for not wanting any awkwardness around the place.

"God, you know how to move, ladies," he announced. "That routine is hot as fuck. I'm feeling a bit nervous now about my band competing against yours."

"If it wasn't for the fact that I can't see you rock gods performing a Jennifer Lopez style dance routine, you'd have been barred from watching," I warned him.

"The very thought." He laughed. It looked good on him. Made his eyes twinkle and his cheeks pink up. But my brain had a hard time adjusting to him not being Noah Granger. *For God's sake, brain.* I was getting increasingly angry at myself. *Just forget him. Forget. Him.*

Of course, as we left the rehearsal space, Noah chose that moment to come walking down the corridor, accompanied by Zak.

"Rivals, see you at showtime." Zak tipped the baseball cap he was wearing.

Noah just narrowed his gaze in Dray's direction. It pissed me off to see his reaction when he hadn't wanted me, so I grabbed Dray's hand. "Shall we grab some beers and burgers at the bar? We have to eat, right?"

"If that's the only thing you're offering up for eating today, a burger it is," Dray growled, pulling me closer to him.

I turned to see Noah's reaction, but he'd gone. Then I got angry at myself for checking in the first place.

I enjoyed my beer and burger. Dray was good company. It was just you never had his attention exclusively. He checked over the barmaid, the other female customers, and no doubt his senses would be on high alert with the audience tonight. He couldn't help it. As shifters, Flame-Grilled Steak all knew their mates were out there somewhere. Dray could offer no woman his heart because it was meant for that mate. But the fact I wasn't his mate wouldn't stop Dray trying to get me horizontal as soon as possible. A topic he seemed to bring up approximately every three minutes.

"Once this competition is over, I just want you to know that I'm gonna be hankering after some of your mighty fine arse, preferably bouncing up and down on my knee, before I spin you around and have you pogo-ing on my cock."

I couldn't help but chuckle. These words somehow came out of his mouth endearingly, even though they were brash and coarse.

"What a romantic," I quipped.

"Can't promise you romance, but I can promise you a good time." He winked.

"Shut up and finish your burger," I told him. Because I knew he told me the truth, and I didn't want to face up to reality right now.

Chapter Twenty-Six

NOAH

"I'm gasping for refreshments and fresh towels," Rex huffed looking from Zak to me. "Can't you two go play a little further afield? We need these people to make sure the show runs smoothly."

"Show's almost over, my friend. And after tonight, Don is going to have me bedding everyone in sight, so if there's anyone you have your eye on or feel a calling to, you'd better give me a heads up," Zak replied.

"Huh, fabulous." Rex threw a drumstick across the room.

"You're just jealous because you have to wait for 'the one'. Your mate. How very boring having to stick to one person for life," Zak teased him.

"Yeah, but until I meet them, I can practice my prowess. That's if there's anyone left after you greedy fuckers have finished." Another drumstick sailed after the first.

"First past the post, my friend."

"Harley's single. I read online that her career comes first but she's not ruling out love," Roman piped up.

"The only person Harley's in love with is herself," Zak answered. "I went full on incubus on her arse and she barely gave me a second glance. She gave the mirrors and windows she passed a lot more attention."

"Is someone a little bitter that there's one woman he's failed to seduce?" I tormented.

"Are you sure she's not a witch?" Zak asked me.

"How should I know?" I became defensive. I couldn't help myself. "Just because my ex was one doesn't mean I have a homing signal for all of their kind."

"You could just ask Stacey."

"Of course I could," I replied sarcastically. "Hey, Stacey, I know we didn't part on the best of terms when I chose the chance of a rock career over you, but could you tell me if Harley is a witch, only we're wondering why she isn't boning Zak?"

"I didn't say you were an expert on witches. I was just pondering whether Harley was one out loud."

"Because she hasn't fallen for your seduction techniques?" I scoffed.

"Yes. I'm an incubus. All human women are supposed to fall at my feet, so that would suggest that she is somehow, something else."

"You're something else," I told him. He stuck his middle finger up at me in response.

It did however get me thinking, because there was still the weird stuff happening that I couldn't explain. Could Harley actually be the cause of it all?

"You're mighty defensive when it comes to talk of Stacey. Has something happened?" Rex asked.

"No," I protested, and as soon as I did, I knew my answer had been a little too quick.

"Noah Granger, you lying bastard. Spill."

Fuck my life, shifters were so damn nosy. They could scent secrets as much as prey.

"We may have spent the night together a few weeks ago," I confessed.

"You devious fucker." Zak stood with his hands on his hips. "So, what happened? And I don't mean between the sheets. Might you two actually sort out your issues?"

"No. Because she'll never forgive me for putting the band before her."

"So do something that puts her before the band," Roman suggested.

Rex and Zak spun their heads towards him as if he'd lost his mind.

"He'd have to quit, dickhead," Zak stated.

I didn't feel like getting into this right now.

"Guys, let's get rehearsing. We've a final to win." I picked up my guitar, and despite receiving a heavy sigh from Roman, we went on to do our final practice of the day.

* * *

Before we knew it, the final was here. We had to sing three songs. Two covers and then one we'd written and done the music for ourselves.

Harley went on stage. She announced the judges who made their grand entrance and took their seats and then the show was underway. The show was live, but on a delay so they could edit where needed, mainly in case someone said something they shouldn't, like Marianne had previously.

"First up tonight is Bill's remaining act The Paranormals." A deafening roar came from the audience. "What have they chosen as their first song of the evening?" she asked him.

Bill leaned over to the microphone. "Well, Harley, let's face it. Every performance from these guys has been incredible. I mean, just look at them." He gestured with his hand. "They already look like they are playing a sell-out gig, not that they're just in the final of a competition. But for our first song we decided they'd sing Bruno Mars, *Marry you.*"

And then we were on stage. The audience screamed their approval, so loud that you couldn't hear the opening bars. Our song was the perfect choice because there wouldn't be a female or male watching who wouldn't be imagining Zak Jones singing directly to them. My eyes flitted out over the audience, and I saw Erica enraptured, bless her. Bill had sent her tickets for the final. Her friend Freya was craning her head towards the back. Yep, she definitely liked our Rex. Shame he was destined for a mate, and if she was it, Rex would already have felt it. This was how it would be now. Meeting women who thought they had a chance with us, when most of the time they wouldn't. As much as being in this competition would bring good things, it would bring an equal amount of trouble. My mind went back to Stacey and how Erica had said we looked good together. We were good together. Goddamn it. They said the path of true love never ran smooth. Our path was littered with obstacles.

As soon as we'd finished, every member of the audience was on their feet. A complete standing ovation.

Harley walked back out onto the stage and beckoned for us to stand at the side of her.

"Okay, guys, that's your first performance of the evening and I think the audience liked it." There were more screams. "Now let's see what the judges thought, starting with your mentor, Bill." Harley gestured to him.

Bill looked smug as the camera returned to him.

"Bill, what an opening to the show. You must be ecstatic right now."

Bill looked directly into the camera, holding up his hand. "What can I say? I told you when I first met these guys, they were the ones to watch, and lads, you just owned the stage."

Next, the camera panned to Carmela. She flicked her fringe, pushed out her hand with her painted talons and roared. "I'd marry you, for sure. Wow. What a smoking performance." She fanned herself, while making sure to squeeze her outfit so her boobs popped out more. From there it was Maxwell, the only one who didn't have an act in the final, who said, "You made it your own. It was sensational." Finally, Marianne told us, "The girls at home will love you. You deserve a place in the final performance a million percent."

The audience were still screaming. I looked at my bandmates and every one of their faces held a huge grin. I knew then, that continuing with the competition had been the right thing to do. For them, at least.

Harley turned to us. "I think the judges liked your performance, don't you?" She beamed her large 'teeth-gleaming under the lights' grin.

"It's always fantastic to hear great comments from the judges and we couldn't ask for a better audience," Zak said, blowing a kiss and getting the audience in a frenzy again when Harley had only just got them to quieten down.

She looked out at the audience, smiled, and asked for

quiet again. "So, before the audience all explode again, is there anything anyone else would like to add?"

"Just to pick up the phone and vote for us," I said.

That was it. The audience were once again deafeningly loud, and you could hardly hear Harley as we left the stage.

"Did you see that?" Zak was bouncing off the walls. "Oh my god, the audience were insane. I think we might actually win this thing."

"Steady on, Zak." I was excited myself, but I didn't want us heading for a huge disappointment. "There are two other really good bands against us."

"Ugh, I can tell you're a vampire, because you suck the life out of anyone's joy." He clapped my back. "We're in the final, my friend. For fuck's sake, enjoy it, and please stop looking like it's the end of days."

"Yes, Noah, enjoy yourself," a familiar voice came from the doorway, and I spun around to find Mya standing there.

"How did you get past secur—" I stopped when I realised the answer. Compulsion.

"Sorry, I'm late. I watched your first act on my phone on the way, but I'm here now."

"Where's Mr Chirpy?" Zak snarked.

"De-nny is around. He'll say hi later," Mya said. "Okay, well good luck, boys, and I'll catch you after the show."

She disappeared at superspeed, and we watched as Seven Sisters took to the stage.

The beginning notes of *Since u Been Gone* by Kelly Clarkson started up. Mmm, I couldn't help but think this was entirely targeted in my direction, and also would help the band as the viewers speculated that it was part of the feud between us. Stacey's vocals were amazing as always, but something seemed off. She didn't seem her usual self. In fact, the band themselves as a whole had a weird vibe.

They still however did a fabulous performance and got great praise from the judges, with the exception of Bill, who played up to his nasty reputation by saying he felt it wasn't the right song choice.

When Harley asked the band what they thought, Donna took the mic off her and told him that he obviously needed a hearing aid.

I saw the shock in Stacey's face at her bandmate's outburst.

Bill shrugged it all off as a joke and Seven Sisters left the stage.

* * *

I'd never really thought of Flame-Grilled Steak as our main competition. Dray and his band were talented, but they didn't hold a candle to Seven Sisters or us. But you should never underestimate the underdogs, especially when they're competitive shifters.

They swaggered onto the stage and began singing their chosen track, The Rolling Stones *(I Can't Get No) Satisfaction*. They'd performed most of the song when suddenly the band placed down their instruments. The audience went quiet, looking at each other wondering what was going on. Marianne, whose band it was, stared smugly at the other judges as their expressions of 'what's happening' struck their faces, even though we knew that nothing that went on stage hadn't been totally agreed beforehand.

And then Flame-Grilled steak began to dance. They took off their shirts, turned and shook their arses, and ran their hands down their body like they were in Magic Mike and the crowd went insane.

Stacey was standing a few people away from me and I turned and looked at her. Her cheeks were puce, and she shook with anger. "Betrayed again. Yet another man puts his music before me. The absolute bastard." She stomped off, one of the other band members trailing after her. Dray would be lucky if that was the only cursing she did after his performance.

With one song down each, there was still everything to play for. But rather than be focusing on our next performance, all I could think about was Stacey.

There was a live performance from Carmela up next,

so while I had the opportunity, I decided I'd go and check on my ex.

But it wasn't to be.

"Right, lads." Bill came walking towards us. The guy had a presence and seemed to bring a sense of power in with him, but he didn't smell of magic. It just seemed to be a genuine charisma. "That stunt Marianne pulled. I knew it was coming, but honestly, I thought they'd look ridiculous. Didn't expect it to be such a success, so what are we going to do to get this back on track and you winning this thing?"

Rex opened his mouth, no doubt to make a suggestion, but Bill was talking rhetorically. "I'll tell you what. You're going to sing *Stay* by Shakespear's Sister as if it's the last song you'll ever sing to your terminally ill wife on her death bed. I want collapsing on your knees and tears streaming down your cheeks, Zak. Then the others come crowd round you. Let the audience think there's been some past lost love and the song has reminded you of it. Okay?"

"Will it get me women falling at my feet?" Zak asked.

"They'll be queuing, mate."

"Done. Prepare to send it for consideration for a BAFTA." He shook Bill's hand and we got quickly changed. Then we were back and they were calling our name to take to the stage.

Chapter Twenty-Seven
STACEY

"I'm going to kill him." I was pacing backstage. "They stole our signature moves. He watched us at the rehearsal, and he pinched our idea, transferred what we were going to do with the final song into their first song."

"So now what do we do?" Meryl asked.

"We carry on as planned, but we take our dance out. Instead, this is what we'll do." I explained my plan. "I'm going to quickly run it past Carmela."

I noticed Donna was keeping quiet. I'd planned on calling her out on her ridiculous outburst until Drayton had pulled that stunt. Now there just wasn't time and I had to hope she kept her mouth shut from now on except for singing.

We made our way back to the stage where The Paranormals had just walked back on. I watched from the shadows. Zak Jones worked the audience like he was a snake charmer, and they were a pit full of adders, but my eyes kept straying to the guy on bass guitar. The first time I let my eyes wander, his gaze snapped to mine, and I realised my guard was down. Fuck. I quickly shut my mind down, locking it in a vault he had no access to. His eyes seemed to dull, and he returned to giving his all to his performance.

They were singing an emotive song, and the audience were mesmerised. Marianne was wiping her eyes. Once again, The Paranormals had pulled ahead of us, with a performance that went beyond an act in a final of a talent competition. Part of me just felt like walking away.

But the other part of me now wanted us to at least wipe out Flame-Grilled Steak from the competition. So we needed to sing our hearts out.

"Come on. Let's make sure that the next performance is Flame-Grilled Steak's final performance."

"Yes, let's," Donna added, and she held up a hand to high five us all.

We sang Pat Benatar's *Love Is A Battlefield* next. We rocked the audience, and you could tell our performance was electric because we were all sharing secret smiles as the crowd got up and danced along. We kept the small dance we had for this one, all of us doing a solo dance move in turn.

We had great feedback from the judges, and I had to

hope it had been enough. Because now Flame-Grilled Steak were coming back out and I had no idea what they were going to do.

* * *

Seemed like most of Flame-Grilled Steak had no idea too...

I stood backstage near the monitors and near The Paranormals and waited for Dray to walk on.

"What the actual fuck?" Zak stated.

Their drummer shrugged his shoulders as they walked past. "We don't know what's going on. He's adamant this is what he's doing. We're fucked."

Dray pranced onto the stage with my fishnet tights on his legs. He'd hacked through them, and they were half hung down because of course otherwise he wouldn't have got them anywhere near his bulky frame. He'd put make-up on to look like mine and a purple wig he'd obviously got from wardrobe. He'd cut his jeans into jean shorts with half his arse hanging out at the back.

Half of the audience were stunned, the other half in hysterics.

The production crew ran around panicking. "We can't let him go on stage like that."

But no one could stop one determined lead singer, not when he was a giant bear of a man. He took to the stage, cued the music and began to sing Rod Stewart's *Da Ya*

Think I'm Sexy... in my higher notes. He sounded like a strangled cat.

"What the actual fuck is happening? Someone tell me." My mouth hung open.

"He wanted to copy us," Donna stated matter of factly. "I gave him a little help."

She said some words of magic and we watched as Dray first looked confused and then down at himself. The crew obviously then managed to get him to listen to instructions in his earpiece as he bolted off stage. Their lead guitarist took over the microphone.

"My apologies. Drayton has been taken ill, which just goes to show that even the most alpha looking of males can at times be vulnerable with their mental health. If these issues affect you, please consult your doctor. Now, if it's okay with everyone, can we start again? I can do the vocals."

They got a thumbs up from the crew and then they sang their song, but the lead guitarist didn't hold the same allure as their lead singer. It was good, but it wasn't final good.

I turned to Donna. "I'm not sure that we can in all good faith join in a final when we cheated our way to it."

"Stacey, what did Dray do? You take this 'do no harm' shit too far. We all have an element of bad in us, it's natural. We don't sign up to practice our craft and then become Mother fucking Teresa. I'm going to get a drink.

I'll be back for the results." Once more Donna walked away from us. She was really starting to piss me off.

"What's with her?" I asked Shonna.

"Fucked if I know," she replied.

* * *

The judges had been supportive with their feedback of Flame-Grilled Steak's performance and gave their best wishes to Dray. Marianne no longer looked so smug. On a final show, judges were never too mean, so they'd not been critical of the stand-in lead's performance.

Harley spoke to the camera announcing that the rest of the final would take place after the evening news, and that was it. We had a short break in proceedings before we'd find out who won Britain's Best New Band.

I turned to walk back to my dressing room, but a tall, pale man blocked my way. Noah passed me a bottle of water.

I took it. "Thanks."

"Nice touch with Dray. I gather you're no longer seeing him." His eyes bored into mine.

"I didn't do it actually. I'm going to go check the guy is okay now, and in answer to your question we were never anything serious. He was good company. Sometimes you need a friend."

"Stacey, I—"

A crew member interrupted us. "They need some shots of you all backstage for the after-show on ITV2."

That was the excuse I needed. I ran ahead of the crew and away from Noah and whatever he wanted to say, because now was not the time, not when either of us might be about to win a lifechanging competition where our lives once more would move in different directions.

* * *

The three of our bands stood side by side on the stage with our mentors as Harley got ready to announce who had made it through to the final two acts.

"I can now announce, the first band through to the final round is..." She paused for what seemed like several years. "The Paranormals."

The audience shrieked and I watched as Noah and his band jumped up and down hugging each other. After he'd gathered himself, his eyes sought mine. I looked away.

Harley got ready to stop one bands journey towards a recording contract. "Okay, if we can have silence now please. The second act through to the final round is..."

Please. Please. Please. Please. Please.

"Seven Sisters."

My bandmates squealed. My own reaction was more one of relief, but I couldn't help but be carried by the happiness of my band, and joy filled my body.

I could feel Noah's gaze on me again. *For heaven's sake, stop,* I mentally begged him, letting my guard down so he could hear my thoughts.

"Flame-Grilled Steak, come gather around me, boys. It's time to take a look at your best bits," Harley stated and the rest of us piled off stage.

* * *

"Stacey," Noah's voice shouted out from behind.

I spun around. "Noah, for God's sake. We're about to sing our final songs, can you leave me alone?"

"I don't want to leave you alone, Stacey. I love you."

He... *what?*

I should have been ecstatic to hear those words. Instead, he'd pissed me right off.

"Now? Now you announce you love me? Just before you might win the record deal with the bandmates you ditched me for?"

"You said you wanted me to choose. I'm sorry for everything that went on before." He grabbed my hand. "I choose you, Stacey. I'll walk away right now. I'll get on that stage and tell everyone, the crowd and the audience of millions, that I'm walking away from the band and walking towards the love of my life."

I snatched my hand back. "I'm not having this conversation right now. Don't be stupid and get ready to sing. I want to beat you."

His eyes bored into mine and he spoke softly. "What for? Why did you enter this competition? You wanted to face me, beat me, and why? I'll tell you why. Because you wanted me to realise what I'd been missing. I can see that, Stacey. I've known since I walked away and I'm here, in front of you. You don't have to beat me."

"Yes, she does." Donna stepped forward. "Because regardless of her intentions for entering, she has six band-mates who are in this with her. You might want to remember your own."

Zak stepped forward from behind Noah. He shrugged his shoulders. "We don't actually give a toss. Clear to see our guy loves your girl. He's a great guitarist, but we could get another one. I'm sure the one from Flame-Grilled Steak would jump right now."

"I think I'm saying 'thanks'." Noah gave Zak a withering gaze.

"I wish I could have one woman for the rest of my life, instead of thousands," Zak added, sighing. Then he pulled a grimace. "Did you hear what I just said?" He pushed Donna on the shoulder. "You put a spell on me or something?"

"Touch me again, I'll put my fist in your balls," she snarked.

"Oooh you like it rough?" Zak's eyes twinkled with mischief.

The production manager came forward. "It's time to sing."

Noah looked at me.

"We'll talk *after* the competition, Noah. I want to know who'd win."

He smiled. "That's not a fuck off. I'll take it."

I smirked and walked away.

I wanted to jump for joy but I kept it cool. Noah loved me! He'd have walked away from it all and he loved me!

Chapter Twenty-Eight

NOAH

This was it, the final of the competition, and... I couldn't give a toss if we won. I thought I had a chance with Stacey.

"Oooooph." I clutched my balls, seeing stars.

Looking up once my vision cleared, I stared straight into the eyes of... Roman??? Jesus, he was the last person I expected to knee me in the nuts.

"You might get your girl. It's all your dreams come true. Fantastic. Guess what my dream is? Winning this competition. So get your focus on going out there and playing that guitar like your life depends on it, because it does. Screw up and I'll fucking kill you."

"Whoa. Listen to goat-boy go. Oooooph." Zak had suffered a similar fate.

Roman turned to Rex, head tilted.

"I ain't got nothing to say except let's do this. I'd like to keep my balls bruise free thanks."

"Let's win this thing!" Roman yelled.

We all high-fived.

It was down to fate now. The competition, my love life. Time to go enjoy our time on stage and see where it took us.

* * *

Harley came out on stage. "Our first act in the final is The Paranormals."

We walked out and sang our song. We gave it everything we had.

Then Seven Sisters came out and did the same.

It was all down to the public now, and who they wanted as Britain's Best New Band.

* * *

This was it. We were on stage to find out who had won. I looked out into the audience. I could see Erica and Freya. I could see Mya and Death. I could see an audience full of screaming supporters.

If my heart beat it would have been thumping now.

My eyes begged me to look at Stacey, but I wouldn't. Not until the announcement. Not until I either rushed to congratulate her or told her I'd leave again. That I chose her.

Harley asked for the audience to be quiet.

"Before we announce the winners, we'd just like to take a few moments to remind you of Dan Trent, who should have been here with me sharing the stage this evening. We haven't given up hope on you, Dan. Please if you're out there watching. Get in touch."

"Like you give a shit, you fame hungry whore," shot out of Bill's mouth.

The audience gasped. Harley froze and Bill laughed like a madman. Getting up from his seat, he walked over and up to Harley's side. He snatched the microphone from her and stood in the centre of the stage.

"This is my show. I'll announce the winner." He listened to his earpiece.

"The winner of tonight's final is…"

The music started up, but now both of our bands were looking at each other, mouthing 'What's happening?'.

"Oh no," Donna shouted.

"What?" Stacey snapped.

"It's… Dan. I think it's Dan. In Bill's body. He would say that. He would say fame hungry whore. Somehow, I must have let him in."

"Me," Bill/Dan announced. "The winner is me. Who cares about the bands? I'm going home to sit by a pool with multiple prostitutes and a mountain of crack, both arse and the white stuff."

The crowd went insane, booing and trying to get at the stage.

And then Death came up with Mya in tow.

"We aren't filming anymore, are we?" I shouted at the others. "Please tell me supernatural identities are not being revealed live on ITV."

"No, they cut us off straight after Bill called me a whore," Harley stated and then Bill/Dan grabbed her by the throat.

"If I'm dead then why should you live?" he whined.

Mya swept forward and pulled his hand away. Stacey dashed towards a spluttering Harley, and then Donna rushed over. "Can someone help me? I accidentally unleashed him. It's the spirit of Dan Trent."

Mya looked shocked. Her eyes widened and she grabbed hold of 'Bill's' throat.

"Is that true? Is that you, Dan? I thought I warned you before. I should have known you'd be a nuisance." She turned to Death. "Take him."

Death walked forward and placed a hand on 'Bill's' forehead.

He uttered words in no language I knew, and then said. "Daniel Trent, leave this body now. You will be sent straight to the Home of Wayward Souls."

"Do not pass Go," Zak yelled before guffawing.

I elbowed him in the ribs.

"Ouch. God, it had to be said. It was too good an opportunity to miss," he complained.

We knew Dan had gone when Bill's face turned pale and he collapsed. Unfortunately, Dan had one last parting shot.

He'd turned to where Stacey was comforting Harley and he'd pushed them. Harley managed to right herself, but Stacey stumbled and fell clean off the stage.

Vampiric speed had never been so welcomed. I got to her within a foot of the floor and threw her up onto the stage. She'd have bruises, but she'd survive.

I wasn't sure I would. Some of the surging angry crowd had tried ripping up floorboards and a sharp upturned piece of wood was about to go through me. I felt it push through my chest and I waited to combust to dust.

Chapter Twenty-Nine
STACEY

I rolled across the stage floor, smarting as my bony bits hit, but then I flew up, my only thoughts of Noah being okay.

However, as I looked over the stage all I could see was a group of people, one of them Mya who was shouting, "Noah, oh fuck, Noah."

Harley grabbed me. "He's okay. I don't know if I am though because I'm seeing some weird shit this evening and I'm wondering if I've been slipped something."

"No, it's real," I told her, and I ran down to where I realised Noah lay on the ground. A piece of wood had gone through his chest and must have just missed his heart. Mya was carefully extracting it, and as it finally came out with a resounding pop that made me feel sick, the gap closed and healed up.

"Oh thank God. My son, I thought you were going to

leave me." She began to cry, which was disconcerting as red tears tracked down her cheeks.

Death joined her. "We need to go, Mya. We have to deal with Dan."

She looked up at him, her fangs bared. "I hate you."

Death just shrugged. "You're the Queen of the Wayward, so tough titty."

"Let me have a moment alone with my son," she commanded. Everyone stepped back including me. "And you, Stacey. This concerns you."

* * *

With everyone rushing around trying to deal with the aftermath of the final going haywire, I sat alongside Noah and Mya on the floor at the front of the stage.

"So Dan *was* killed," Noah said. "Shit, wonder what happened there?"

"I drained him," Mya said, looking at her fingernails as if she hadn't just confessed to murder.

She looked up and caught mine and Noah's wide-eyed expressions. "Oh, his time was up. Death told me. He accidentally said it while we were watching the auditions. Told me he'd seen his name on the board. Was gonna get hit by a bus. Anyway, I secretly came to the earlier auditions to keep an eye on you two, and I saw him threaten Harley. Said if she didn't leave, he would... well, it wasn't nice stuff he threatened to do with her. His aura was all off, he smelled bad. He'd have done something evil. So I offed him a week early."

Noah sighed. "Mya, did you by any chance have anything to do with the disappearance of Jack Brooks?"

"What?" I half-shouted.

Mya just shrugged. "He was another one. When they're truly evil I can smell them; they're like really bad diarrhoea after sprouts. I couldn't stop Stacey giving away her virginity, she did that freely, but he was going to attack her after." She looked at me. "He was going to hurt you, and then go on to hurt others before taking the cowards way out when caught, so I did the world a favour."

"Mya, you can't just go around draining people," I said.

"I'm a vampire queen, sweetpea, that's exactly what I can do." She patted my hair. "Bless."

Rising to her feet, she knocked dust off the back of her dress. "Right, me and Death need to get moving. I'm hoping you two can finally stop wasting time, although you're going become a vampire and live with him forever now. I've seen the entry where your human life ends in The Book of the Dead."

"MYA," Death shouted. "The book is confidential. How many more times?"

"Oops, I'm in trouble again. Hopefully I'll get

punished." She winked, kissed our cheeks, went to Death's side and then they were gone.

We realised the hysteria surrounding us.

"I need to do my bit," Noah said, and he whizzed to the stage.

I guessed what he was going to do, and sure enough, he held the audience, staff, and judges in a huge compulsion, clearing their minds off anything that had happened.

The power of suggestion meant that everyone believed an overwhelmed Bill had suffered a breakdown on live TV. A production member then added that a substitute programme had hastily been added to the schedule.

The production team gathered the members of the two bands together and Bill himself came to find us. He looked a lot better, though shellshocked.

"Look, darlings, I'm not sure what happened this evening, but it's clear I've obviously been working myself into the ground. Anyhow, the results came in at a dead heat. It's never been known. With that in mind you'll both be joining my team. Someone will be in touch, okay?"

I looked across at Noah. "Seven Sisters would have won if there was one more voter."

He looked back at me. "Come on, Stace, give it up. It's a dead heat. We drew. Can we finally call a truce?"

I took a deep breath. Now I needed to decide what my future held. Were music and Noah a part of it?

Chapter Thirty
MYA

On my way out of the building with Death I'd passed Bill. "Just a minute, sweetie. I need a quick word with him."

Death sighed heavily but stood still and folded his arms over his chest.

I got the medics standing with Bill to move away with a kind word in their ears (aka the power of suggestion) and then I looked deep into Bill's eyes.

"You will cancel the phone vote and refund every penny, and you will believe regardless of the results that it was a dead heat."

He nodded.

No one would ever know who actually won the competition.

No one. Not even me.

Are you annoyed? Now you know what my mood was like when someone turned me into a vampire and made me Queen of the Wayward.

Fucking infuriating, isn't it?

Chapter Thirty-One
NOAH

Bill walked away, the production crew left us, and our two bands sat dumbstruck. It was an expression we'd worn on more than one occasion that evening.

Harley walked in with a bottle of champagne in each hand and passed one to Roman, and one to Donna.

I'd just asked Stacey what was happening now, but as Roman popped the cork and my bandmates started jumping around, I once again realised that this wasn't the time either. Maybe there'd never be a right time. Donna dragged Stacey by the hand, and they popped the cork of their bottle. Then champagne was being shaken and poured over all of us and we began to realise we'd won a fucking recording contract.

"Let's move this party somewhere better," Donna said.

"I know just the place," Zak answered.

And with that we all set off for Sheol.

* * *

I watched from the edge of the dance floor as Stacey moved her hips to the beat of the music. She raised her hands and swayed, while around her, her bandmates made similar moves. But I wasn't interested in them.

The Paranormals had celebrated our future with shots, and as a bevvy of females began to keep approaching us, we realised that life was about to change. Don had sent Aaron down to make sure no one harmed his incubus. Zak was going to be a busy boy.

Aaron walked over to me, and no one was more surprised than me when he spoke.

"You need to stop staring at her and go get her. Don't take no for an answer. You're a vampire. A predator. Why are you not claiming her as your own?"

"I don't know, Aaron," I admitted honestly. "When it comes to Stacey, I'm weak."

"We're all weak when it comes to love," he said. "Even demons."

He looked over at Zak, who was charming the ladies, but who wore a tormented expression around his eyes.

I realised that Aaron was telling me something.

"Us demons learn certain information at each level,

but as I'm working for the big, bad boss, I'm privy to more information than I should know. If he finds out I've told you, I'll be incinerated, but I have a son Zak's age, and I can't imagine him being bound to a life like Zak's." He took a deep breath. "When he finds true love, his contract ends. His soul will be returned."

I gasped.

"But you can't tell him that. To tell him would be to torment him. He'd be unlikely to find it if too focused. And more than that, it would mean a disqualification. He wouldn't be able to end his contract with Don."

"But I can try to help him look for love, albeit discreetly?"

"As long as you don't tell him the truth."

I patted Aaron on the arm. "Thank you, Aaron. Thank you so much."

Aaron nodded his head and began to walk away, and then he turned back around. "She's looked over here at least six times while we've been talking. If you let her leave this time, it will be the end of this. I can see it in her eyes."

I remembered what Zak had said about being able to find another bass guitarist if needed. I realised that was fine with me.

Oh I'd be crushed for a while. Music had been my dream, but Stacey... Stacey was reality, and right now, it was time to do what I did best.

Stalk and claim my prey.

* * *

I waited for Stacey to walk down the corridor towards the ladies bathrooms and then I swiftly grabbed her and pulled her into a dark alcove of the club at lightning speed. The scream was only just appearing at her lips when she realised who'd done it and where we were.

"For God's sake, Noah. I'm going to need my hairdresser on speed dial at this rate to cover my grey."

"I'm done, Stacey," I told her.

"What?" Her eyes looked panicked.

"With the band. With The Paranormals. I'm done with the band."

"Oh." She let out an exhale.

"Shit, you thought I meant with you."

"Duh," she said, punching me in the chest.

My stomach flipped as I realised she'd have been upset if we were over.

"I'm far from done with you, Stacey Williams. I haven't even started what I intend to do with you."

"Oh yeah? Like what?" She raised a brow.

"I'm going to kiss you, love you, fuck you, make love to you, and marry you, Stacey. That's if you forgive me for the mistakes of my youth. I promise you'll never come second in my life ever again."

"I'll consider this on one condition." Stacey folded her arms across her chest.

"Okay, what is it?"

"You take the recording contract and see where your music takes you."

I shook my head. "No, Stacey..."

She raised a hand and put her fingers across my lips. "Noah, I asked you to choose, and you did. You chose me. You would put me before everything. That's all I've ever thought I wanted, but actually it's selfish. I couldn't live with myself knowing I stopped your dreams. We'd not survive that."

I smirked.

"Yeah, okay, you're dead anyway and I'm apparently going to become a vampire, so neither of us is surviving, but you get my gist."

"I do."

"I've realised there are things I need to do for myself. I quite fancy being a theatre actress down the line. Therefore, I've decided that I'm going to tour with whoever of the Seven Sisters wants to and see what opportunities it brings. I spoke to Harley, and she says it's going to be a joint tour with two headline acts."

"Looks like we're stuck with each other for a while then." My smile broke across my face, and I swear it almost cracked my jaw it was so wide.

"Yep, sure looks that way." Stacey smiled back. "Now what did you say you were going to do with me again?"

"I think I started with kiss you," I said, and I leaned forward and claimed her mouth with my own.

Chapter Thirty-Two

Erica

From: TheSubsofTheParanormals@gmail.com
Subject: EXCLUSIVE – EXCLUSIVE – EXCLUSIVE – OMG THEY GOT MARRIED!
Date: 20 May 2023

From the ONLY OFFICIAL fan group of The Paranormals.

OMFG Subs!

They only went and did it in secret!

Noah Granger and Stacey Williams are now man and wife! Photos are being released to the press, but here's one they sent especially for the Subs along with this sweet message.

Subs,
We couldn't wait any longer and didn't need a fancy ceremony. All we need is each other.
Now we're Mr & Mrs Granger and couldn't be happier.
We look forward to seeing you on tour soon. Don't forget to grab your tickets as from September, Stacey will be leaving The Seven to star in the West End as Velma in Chicago.
There's no time for a honeymoon, but we're okay with that. We're enjoying singing our music to you all.
Thanks for all your support. You're the best!
Noah & Stacey (Mr & Mrs Granger) xo

I have it on good authority that Donna Matthews will be taking over the lead. I have to say when I first heard a few of Seven Sisters weren't going ahead with the tour, I was worried as you know, but then three of Flame-Grilled Steak joined them and now I think The Seven are amazing.

I asked Charlie from FGS how Dray was doing and apparently, he met his 'one' in hospital and he's home and living happy ever after so that's good news isn't it?

Anyway, I'll leave you to celebrate the exciting news and I'll be in touch with you soon, when I'll have an exclusive interview with our lead singer. Yes, Zak Jones will be talking to me. Is this real life? Where I get up close and personal with The Paranormals?

Happy sigh.

Erica xoxo

* * *

I proofread the piece and then I pressed send to the thousands of subscribers. It grew day by day. The Seven did well, but The Paranormals were becoming superstars.

They were so busy that now I dealt with their PA, Vikki.

I began to write my list of questions for Zak. I'd send them to Vikki and she'd send me the answers back. It was just like backstage on Britain's Best New Band. To the Subs, it looked like I was living my dreams, speaking to the hottest band of the moment regularly, but in reality, I was nowhere near them.

And I so wanted to be near Zak Jones. Preferably underneath him.

I sighed as I clicked onto the showbiz pages where I looked at him with woman after woman after woman.

Seemed some things just weren't meant to be.

*   *   *

I met Freya. We'd decided to have a meal at the Rock Hard Bistro where Stacey used to work. Their food was amazing, and the atmosphere was great.

We'd just taken our seats when a woman came rushing over to us, followed by an older lady.

"Ebony, can we not have this every time you visit?" the older woman yelled.

The woman grabbed my arm. I flinched, but then she said. "You must follow your heart. Don't give up on your dreams of love."

Her perfectly enunciated words, said in a cut-glass accent that sounded like the tinkle of piano keys, took away the shock of her having grabbed my arm.

The older woman pulled her away and apologised.

I said it was fine. And it really was.

Because my heart belonged to Zak Jones, and now I would go follow him.

THE END

Can Zak find true love and end his demonic contract? Find out in ROCK 'N' SOULS.

Read Mya's story in SUCK MY LIFE.

If you enjoyed HEX FACTOR please consider leaving a review.

To keep up with latest release news and receive an exclusive subscriber only ebook DATING SUCKS: A Supernatural Dating Agency prequel short story, sign up here: geni.us/andiemlongparanormal

Playlist

Taylor Swift, *Wildest Dreams*
Britney Spears, *Toxic*
Britney Spears, *Womanizer*
Kelly Clarkson, *Since u Been Gone*
Rolling Stones, *(I Can't Get No) Satisfaction*
Bruno Mars, *Marry You*
Pat Benatar, *Love Is A Battlefield*
Rod Stewart, *Da Ya Think I'm Sexy*

About Andie

Andie M. Long's love of vampires, reading, and her wicked sense of humour resulted in her creating her own paranormal comedy worlds.

She lives in Sheffield.

When not being partner, mother, or writer, she can usually be found on social media, at her allotment, or walking her whippet, Bella. She's addicted to coffee, chocolate, and Vinted.

Andie also writes contemporary romance under the penname Angel Devlin and psychological suspense as Andrea M. Long.

* * *

ABOUT ANDIE

SOCIAL MEDIA LINKS

Follow me on TikTok and Instagram:
@andieandangelbooks

Join my reader group on Facebook:
www.facebook.com/groups/haloandhornshangout

Paranormal Romance
By Andie M. Long

PARANORMAL ROMANTIC COMEDY TITLES

SUPERNATURAL DATING AGENCY

The Vampire wants a Wife
A Devil of a Date
Hate, Date, or Mate
Here for the Seer
Didn't Sea it Coming
Phwoar and Peace
Acting Cupid
Cupid Fools
Dead and Breakfast
A Fae Worse than Death

Also on audio, paperback, and series bundles available.

SUPERNATURAL ROCK STARS

Hex Factor
Rock 'n' Souls
We Wolf Rock You
Satyrday Night Fever

Also in paperback. Complete series volume available.

* * *

SUCKING DEAD

Suck My Life – available on audio.
My Vampire Boyfriend Sucks – available on audio.
Sucking Hell – available on audio
Suck it Up
Hot as Suck
Just my Suck
Too Many Sucks
Sucking Nightmare

* * *

OTHER PARANORMAL ROMANCE TITLES

PARANORMAL ROMANCE BY ANDIE M. LONG

DARK AND TWISTED FAIRY TALES

Caging Ella
Sharing Snow

* * *

Filthy Rich Vampires – Reverse Harem
Royal Rebellion (Last Rites/First Rules duet) – Time Travel Young Adult Fantasy
Immortal Bite – Gothic romance

Printed in Great Britain
by Amazon

96181e1b-2795-40a6-b78a-906ff0308eecR01